Within the Walls

WITHIN THE WALLS

A Journey Through Sexism and
Racism in Corporate America

DAISY M. JENKINS

Within the Walls: A Journey Through Sexism and Racism in Corporate America

Published by Wheatmark®
1760 East River Road, Suite 145
Tucson, Arizona 85718 USA
www.wheatmark.com

ISBN: 978-1-62787-206-5 (paperback)
ISBN: 978-1-62787-207-2 (ebook)
LCCN: 2014952935

This book is dedicated to the memory of my parents, Mr. Isiah Bell and Mrs. Daisy Bell, and my mother-in-law, Mrs. Jimmie Gipson Loftis. They endured the degradation of Jim Crow laws, verbal and physical abuse, and countless indignities of second-class citizenship so that my generation could have access to the opportunities that eluded their generation. They didn't experience the dignity of being properly addressed by their last name, with a handle ("Mr." or "Mrs.") outside the Black community. Instead, they heard only Isiah, Daisy, and Jimmie.

They lived by the old African proverb "It's not what you call me but what I answer to." Thank God for their strength and their character.

Contents

1   Hillary: Lord, Get Me Through This; Rejection Is Hell   1

2   Darryl: I Deserve the Best and Nothing Less!   12

3   Hillary: Another Day of Disappointment!   23

4   Darryl: Driving While Black Is Hazardous to Your Health   34

5   Lucia: Some Things Just Don't Make Sense   46

6   Hillary: Hallelujah, My Time Has Come!   54

7   Darryl: They Finally Got It Right!   59

8   Hillary: I Love My New Job!   65

9   Lucia: Best Friends Forever   70

10   Darryl: My Plans Are Falling into Place   75

11   Hillary: I Can't Believe My Ears   79

12   Darryl: The Payback Plans Continue   84

13   Lucia: How Do We Outsmart the Schemers?   90

14   Darryl: Keeping Everything on Track   96

15   Hillary: Mr. Darryl Kelsey, Who Do You
     Think You Are?   101

16   Lucia: The Project of a Lifetime   106

17   Darryl: The Hour Draws Near   114

18   Darryl: One Down, One to Go   119

19   Lucia: The Devil Is in the Details   132

20   Darryl: Oh, What a Relief It Is   139

21   Hillary: That's What Friends Are For   151

22   Lucia: Preparing for the Big Meeting   157

23   Darryl: I Haven't Changed That Much!   161

24   Lucia: The Castillo Team Visits   168

25   Darryl: Revenge Is Near   178

26   Hillary: I'm Scared to Death!   185

27   Darryl: Oh, What a Night!   192

28   Hillary: Am I Really Going to Be Cured?   207

29   Darryl: It's Time for a Change   215

30   Lucia: Mexico, Here We Come!   225

31   Darryl: It Is Possible to Change   238

32   Hillary: God Never Fails!   252

33   Darryl: The Big Showdown   260

34   Hillary: All's Well That Ends Well   268

Acknowledgments   279

1 HILLARY

Lord, Get Me Through This;
Rejection Is Hell

The early-morning sun sends sparkling waves of light dancing in unison through my bedroom window, as if choreographed to wake me for a day of new possibilities. I arise with mixed feelings of excitement and fear.

Today I have my sixth job interview in four weeks, and thoughts of doom are already racing through my head. I'm so fearful it will be another day of rejection and disappointment. Will I once again fail to measure up to the unpredictable hiring standards of another corporation—standards often based more on my physical appearance and other superficial measures than on my experience and professional competencies?

Here I am, with a college degree from a reputable university, and I'm being rejected for administrative assistant positions that don't even *require* a college degree. They tell me I either am overqualified or don't have enough experience in a specific area (usually an obscure experience not mentioned in the job description). There's always a cheerful reminder they'll "keep my resume on file" and a promise I'll be a "top contender" for a future opening in my field.

This repeated rejection has taken a toll on both my self-esteem and my confidence. I keep questioning my abilities. Yet I know that I can do these jobs with my hands tied behind my back. There has to be something that I'm missing that's holding me back.

Just last week, my friend Tesha told me that my natural hairstyle may be the problem, and she added, "It wouldn't hurt for you to shed a few pounds before the next interview." With her tall, shapely body and gorgeous, straight bob, she meant well. But I love my full, natural hair, which has grown to the perfect length. My curls fall into place like they know just where they belong. Besides, I refuse to terrorize my scalp with harsh chemical straighteners that contain lye and other toxins to meet someone else's standard of beauty.

Most of all, I love my hair because it shows who I am. I refuse to compromise my physical characteristics (as many Black people do) to fit into a corporate mold, and yes, I've gained a few pounds. That's another way of saying I'm "well endowed," but I'm not obese. Over the past three months, I've developed a strong relationship with my favorite comfort food—glazed donuts. I have no doubt it results from the stress of having been laid off *and* this unproductive job search.

I lost my job as a project coordinator for a team of accountants just twelve weeks ago. It was totally unexpected, because my supervisor, Doris, had continuously complimented the quality of my work during my two years there. She often told me I was a breath of fresh air compared with the two other coordinators, who took frequent smoke breaks and spent too much time on personal phone calls. But I'm twenty-six and they're forty-seven and fifty-nine, which means they got to stay. It was "hit the road, Jack" for me.

I had taken the coordinator job even though it didn't require a college degree as a foot in the door to a meaningful career in a reputable company. I actually loved and quickly mastered all elements of the job. I absorbed new information like a sponge. So I thought for sure that I was on my way to the next rung up on the career ladder—one more suited to my degree in management information systems.

When Doris called me into her office that Friday morning, I *knew* she was giving me the new assignment that we'd discussed a couple weeks earlier. First, she asked me to have a seat. Then I suddenly felt a sense of dread when I saw the sister from Human Resources sitting next to her.

I also noticed Doris could barely make eye contact with me; instead, she showed me a level of uneasiness I hadn't seen during the past two years. After she said, "Hillary, I regret to inform you that today is your last day at work because of cost-reduction measures," every word that followed was garbled. Doris kept to the Human Resources script, but she was almost in tears. Where was the "human" in this message?

The sister from Human Resources saw Doris's discomfort and took over. She even smiled as she said, "Hillary, the company is generously giving you four weeks of severance to assist in your transition. It's normally only two weeks of severance, but 'we' want to acknowledge your solid performance over the past two years." The smiling sister continued speaking as she said, "There's no need to return to your desk. I'll have someone from Human Resources gather your personal effects and bring them to you in the front lobby."

It took everything within me to control the shaking hands that wanted to reach out and choke her until no breath was left in her body. The smiling sister continued talking. "Hillary, if you have any questions or notice anything missing from your personal effects when you get home, don't hesitate to call the number on this card. Please know that we're here to assist you." She handed me a card (no company logo) with a phone number to call Human Resources. In effect, that told me that, after two noteworthy years, I was now a potential

threat and needed to depart the premises immediately.

The smiling sister continued, "I'll escort you
to the front lobby. We can use the back stairs if
that's more comfortable for you." I saw Doris look
helplessly my way. She kept silent as we departed.
"By the way," the smiling sister said, "here's a severance agreement for you to sign in order to be paid
the four weeks' severance. Feel free to have your
attorney review the agreement before signing, but
rest assured that our legal team carefully drafted
this agreement. Of course, the sooner you sign the
document, the sooner you'll receive the four weeks'
pay."

*How much time would I have to serve in prison if I
pushed her down the stairs?* I could always say it was
an accident, but who would believe that? After all,
she had participated in my layoff notification.

Once we reached the lobby, I knew the
company had me over a barrel. So I signed the
agreement before I left and handed it to the smiling
sister without looking up at her. A guy from Human
Resources handed me my things and nodded with a
smile. The smiling sister had the gall to say, "Hillary,
with your skills, I'm sure you'll find another job
really soon." I hope my nonverbal expression in
that moment conveyed the words that were deeply
embedded in my throat: *I hope you rot in hell.*

I have no idea how I got home that day. Everything blurred when I left the building. It didn't matter that I had been an outstanding employee. To them, my position represented a cost savings of over $55,000 annually, while some of the well-known poorly performing accountants in my department kept their cushy jobs with salaries that tripled mine.

Do they still have those colorful posters on the walls that say OUR PEOPLE ARE OUR GREATEST ASSET? Tell that to the fifty greatest assets who lost their jobs that day. The pain of the inhumanity I experienced still causes rage to boil inside me whenever I allow my thoughts to pause for even a second on that day.

❁ ❁ ❁

My body suddenly shivers as I feel the cold dampness beneath me. Once again, the secret shame that I've experienced since I was a teenager has made its presence known. I've had a few months of dryness, and I didn't think today's interview would cause my problem to resurface. You see, whenever I face a major, stressful situation, my bladder kicks into fifth gear the night before, and I awaken in the morning to soiled, wet sheets.

No one knows why this problem started when it did. I've been to several urologists and psychiatrists, but so far nothing or no one has solved the problem. In high school, that meant no overnight sleepovers with my girlfriends. I'd respond to their invitations with masterful excuses, until the invitations eventually stopped. I have prayed for relief from what should have been an early childhood issue, but even God has turned a deaf ear.

When I began college, my mother, God bless her soul, worked an extra job in addition to my part-time work so I could afford a one-bedroom apartment. I couldn't deal with having a dorm roommate. And instead of partying and going on dates, I immersed myself in learning Spanish, a language that I loved and was determined to master.

So, at twenty-six years old, who am I? A fluent Spanish–speaking adult bed wetter.

Typically, I'd remove the soiled sheets and toss them into the washer. One saving grace is that my small apartment has a large-capacity washer and dryer, which allow this embarrassment to remain a secure secret with me. Thank God my mother helped pay for these appliances. She had her struggles after my father died, but she's been my rock forever, and I can't thank her enough. My father was a wonderful man whom I loved dearly. He passed away when I was thirteen. My mother believes my bed wetting was a reaction to his death. His passing left such a void in my life that, as much as I love my mother, even she couldn't fill it. I'd lie awake at night, thinking about my father, and cry myself to sleep. As time passed, I began waking in the mornings to wet sheets. Maybe my tears were so abundant, they flowed through my body. Anyway, the problem has continued into adulthood.

To this day, my curious and opinionated best friend, Lucia Hernandez, questions me about why I need a large-capacity washer and dryer in my one-bedroom apartment. So far, she's been satisfied with the response that doing laundry only after I accumulate a large load of clothes cuts down on my electric bill. I love that girl, but I know she will continue to ask; Lucia is like a pit bull when she's curious about something. I can't imagine her reaction if she knew the truth.

But that's the least of my worries this morning. This apartment and the washer-dryer won't be mine much longer if I don't land a job soon.

❈ ❈ ❈

My ringing telephone snaps me out of what I call my post-layoff funk, similar to post-traumatic stress disorder. I know I've got to stop torturing myself by recounting over and over the events of that Friday. But it's hard to let go of something that was so devastating to my self-worth, my financial stability, and my professional future.

The caller ID shows my dear mother's name, Linda Montgomery. Mother may live several hundred miles away in Bainbridge, Georgia, but she gives new meaning to being just a phone call away. As soon as I answer the phone, she goes into her barrage of questions. "Hillary, what took you so long to answer the phone? Are you getting ready for the interview? Are you wearing the nice navy suit I bought you with the crisp white blouse? I know you love your natural hair, but do you have the right oil so it doesn't look dull? Have you prayed this morning? Hillary, are you still there?"

I sigh as I respond, "Hi, Mom. I'm getting ready, and I'm wearing the navy suit with the white blouse. My hair is just fine, and I will not go to my interview with my hair dripping oil like the characters in Eddie Murphy's old movie *Coming to America*. I'll call you later; I've got to finish getting dressed. I love you."

"I love you too, baby. My prayer partners have already joined in praying for your interviews. And I have a good feeling that this will be the day for your special blessing. You know, God doesn't always answer us when we want him to, but he's always on time. He's a mighty good God!"

I get an early-morning sermon like this at least four times a week. My mother means well but can be a royal pain in the butt. "Okay, Mom, I've got to go. Talk to you later. Love you. Bye."

❁ ❁ ❁

I collect myself and kneel down next to my bed for morning prayer. "Loving God, thank you for allowing me to see another day. I am in need of your grace and mercy as I go to today's job interview with Sanger International. I know that I'm not worthy, but I need you to open this door for me, if it's your will.

"Lord, I yearn for your will to be that I'm hired for this position. Guide my thoughts and my words. Help me to speak with confidence and competence when I respond to the interview questions. Please send your angels my way to intervene on my behalf on this day. Thank you for your goodness and your many blessings. You said you would never leave me or forsake me, so please be with me today. Forgive my sins and help me always to worship you in spirit and in truth. I love you, Lord, and make these requests in Jesus's name. Amen."

I always feel better after I pray, but I can't help thinking, *I hope God notices that I didn't mention anything this morning about my bladder problem, because I know He's tired of hearing that request.*

❖ ❖ ❖

Even though I'm nervous, I'm also excited about my interview with Sanger International, a top information technology consulting firm. Lucia, who works for the company, urged me to apply for this position. When I got the call for an interview, I literally did cartwheels across the floor. And that's a tremendous feat, especially given the extra pounds I have to throw around.

I rush to take a hot shower with renewed energy and the faith that everything will work out fine. Hearing my mother's voice in my head, I pull out my conservative navy suit and crisp white blouse for the interview, plus my classic navy heels. *At least they can't screen me out because of unprofessional attire.*

After eating a light breakfast, I check the clock. It's already nine. My first interview begins at ten, and I always try to show up at least fifteen minutes ahead of the scheduled interview time. I have a half-hour drive and should meet my timeline once I park the car and walk to the office building.

With the planning done, I say another quick prayer: "Lord, I'm sorry for bugging you again. I thank you for this opportunity and pray that it materializes into meaningful employment. Please guide my thoughts and words so that I demonstrate the utmost poise and confidence. Amen."

I take one last look in my full-length mirror. Mother's correct: Sanger *is* the right place for me. She has powerful prayer partners, and I'm glad they're on their knees for me, for today, I need all the help I can get.

2 DARRYL

I Deserve the Best and Nothing Less!

I can't believe the snarl of traffic this afternoon. It's not rush hour, so what's the problem? My meeting lasted longer than expected, and I have an interview for my executive assistant position at two o'clock. There should be a new local traffic statute making it mandatory for people who work in jobs that pay below a certain level to carpool or ride public transportation. It would help those people save money and would make traffic more manageable for white-collar professionals and executives like me.

And just look at the guy driving an old wreck of a car. I can't believe I have to yield to him in my 2014 Mercedes S550. Give me a break! My traffic statute would also prohibit cars built earlier than 2000 from being driven during the hours when professionals like me are commuting.

I think I'll speak to my councilman about introducing such a bill. After all, I shed out $2,500 for his reelection campaign. Got to stick together with my conservative brethren. They understand the problems that good-for-nothing people are causing us. It's time we get those people under control. They are an embarrassment to the truly hardworking professionals who have pulled ourselves up by our bootstraps. Too many handouts these days are destroying the strength of our nation.

My God, it's one thirty. I have to hurry to get to my office, or I'll be late for the interview. Our new project needs immediate support, so my executive assistant position has to be filled quickly. My team has been interviewing the candidate since ten o'clock this morning. It would be great if the right person showed up today. I can see her now, a beautiful blonde with the brightest blue eyes, 36-24-36, and in awe of a brilliant, handsome man like me. I've told Human Resources they've got to get it right this time, without telling them exactly what I'm looking for. Of course, they should know by now, givens the hints I've provided and the candidates I've turned down. I always get the usual HR speech—"Mr. Kelsey, we must send you the most qualified candidates"—but that's a bunch of bull, and they know it. Some of my colleagues are very specific about whom they will hire—most often, their children, girlfriends, friends, friends' children, and others—and always manage to do so without HR's meddling. My assistant has to be a good fit with my status in the company and must meet or even exceed my expectations.

As I pull into my personal parking space, I notice people checking out my wheels. I imagine they're waiting to see who emerges from this fine car. As the most handsome and sharp-dressed guy at Sanger, I never let anyone down. Today, I'm wearing my black Armani suit with a soft pink shirt and a black-and-pink paisley Versace tie. My black Bally loafers are brilliantly shined to punctuate my attention to detail in every aspect of my life. There's nothing worse than seeing so-called professional men in off-the-rack suits with dusty shoes. Those are the ones I don't want on my team. When I interview male candidates, no matter how smart they are, their shoes have to be shined or they don't get the job. I think the spineless HR liberal, Glenn Hendricks, has been giving dudes a heads-up about my dress code; lately, all the candidates he's sent me have had on spit-shined shoes.

I rush to an elevator filled with employees and punch the button for the twenty-second floor. Why aren't these people at their desks? I avoid making eye contact by always looking upward at the bright elevator lights. It's a different story if one of the other vice presidents is onboard; then I can engage in conversation with an equal. I don't know why Sanger doesn't have a dedicated elevator for vice presidents and above.

My temporary assistant, Gail, greets me with a smile. "Good afternoon, Mr. Kelsey." I nod at her as I enter my office. She's a decent person but definitely doesn't meet my standards for a permanent assistant. It's almost two o'clock, and Gail is on the phone with Human Resources. "Mr. Kelsey, the executive assistant candidate has already arrived. Shall I bring her up now?" I answer, "Get me a latte from Starbucks first, and please rush back so it stays nice and hot." I see the sneer on Gail's face from the mirror mounted in my office that's projected toward my assistant's cubicle.

My desk is covered with papers for the new project. I've got to get an assistant, and I'd love to find *her*—definitely not a him—today.

Gail is literally perspiring as she brings in my latte. She had to trek down three flights of stairs and then run back up with the hot latte. "You can go retrieve the candidate now, and please close the door on your way out," I say. I like the door closed when candidates arrive so they grasp my importance within Sanger. With the door closed, Gail has to notify me on the intercom when the candidate has arrived, as she does with this candidate. "Mr. Kelsey, Ms. Hillary Montgomery is here. Shall I bring her in now?"

In my most confident and authoritative voice, I say, "Yes, please bring in Ms. Montgomery."

Oh hell no! HR has blown it again. Hillary Montgomery is a Black woman! Gail politely asks this candidate, "Ms. Montgomery, may I get you some water or tea?" I still don't understand why Gail has to make this offer, especially to a candidate who won't be here long enough to enjoy a drink.

"No, thank you," responds Ms. Montgomery. At least she doesn't sound ghetto. Gail leaves, closing the door behind her.

I'm in a state of shock and catch myself staring at Hillary Montgomery. She's nicely dressed but definitely doesn't fit the description of my ideal assistant, even though last night I reviewed her resume, which was quite impressive, and found her more than qualified for the position. I had high hopes for this candidate; "disappointed" doesn't begin to describe my reaction. Her nice blue suit, probably purchased on sale at one of the outlet malls, doesn't hide the fact she's overweight. And why the hell didn't she do something with her hair? I can't stand to see Black women with natural hair.

I offer her a chair across from my large desk to ensure the widest distance between us. "Thank you, Mr. Kelsey," she says. "You have a very nice office. I love the decor." *Nice?* She should be saying my office is *awesome.* I'm sure she's never worked for an executive in a space this stylishly decorated.

We go through the typical interview questions: "Tell me about yourself"; "Describe your strengths and areas that need improvement"; "What was the most recent book you read?" I must admit, she answers all of them with poise and confidence, although I can see she's a bit nervous by the way she keeps crossing and uncrossing her legs.

I force a smile when saying, "Ms. Montgomery, tell me about your last job and why you left that position."

"Please, call me Hillary."

I nod but hope she doesn't think I'll ask her to call me Darryl. It's Mr. Kelsey to her and everyone else. I know people think I'm old school because I insist that employees refer to me this way, but they just don't understand the respect that goes along with "Mr. Kelsey," or how important respect is to me.

Hillary continues, "I was laid off from my position because of cost reductions after two years of employment. I was viewed as a high-performing employee, but there were others with more seniority. I really loved the work and had hoped to be a long-tenured employee. It was disappointing, but I guess these things happen."

Who in the hell does she think she's fooling? Companies rarely lay off high-performing employees. She was probably a real slacker. It doesn't make sense to drag out this interview, so I need to bring things to a close. "I'm sorry things didn't work out for you at your last company. We appreciate your interest in Sanger. We'll make a hiring decision soon, and someone from Human Resources will get back to you."

I can sense Hillary's disappointment, but she maintains her composure. "Thank you, Mr. Kelsey. I appreciate the opportunity to interview for this position and hope you'll see my skills and competencies as a good fit for this position. When can I expect to hear from Human Resources?"

To save her from any lost sleep over the decision, I want to say, *Lady, you really don't want to know; there's no way in hell I'm hiring you as my assistant.* Instead, I opted for professionalism and respond, "You should hear something within the next week." She thanks me as she leaves my office, and Gail takes her to the elevator.

Gail can see I'm not a happy camper when she returns. I literally yell out to her, "Gail, tell the team who interviewed Hillary that I want to see them in my conference room, pronto." It doesn't matter what they think of Hillary; she isn't going to get the job. I will, however, go through the motions of asking their opinions.

Once they arrive and are seated around the conference table, I ask for feedback on Hillary's interviews. Each of them, except John Griffin, says she's the ideal candidate and has strong competencies, far above and beyond the skills necessary for my assistant position. It's no surprise that John isn't pleased with her; his comments are true to form when he says, "The 'girl' didn't impress me as meeting the qualifications for the position. She has a degree, but you know how some people get those degrees through degree factories. I don't think hers is legitimate." The truth is, John is never pleased with any candidate who doesn't have white skin.

Let's end this charade, I think. Hillary Montgomery is not right for me, and I say as much. "I think she's okay, but the fact she was laid off from her last job doesn't sit well with me. My sixth sense tells me she might not work out in our environment. I can't take the risk, given the complex projects we're dealing with at this time."

One of my managers, Michael Dunlap, the resident liberal who some people think is a homosexual, has different thoughts. "I really like Hillary and would bring her into my department in a hot minute if she doesn't get hired as your assistant. She's sharp, she has excellent communication skills, and we desperately need someone with her talents."

It's just like Michael to rescue candidates who don't meet my qualifications or high expectations. What's up with these gays and liberals? I don't care if he wants her, as long as I don't have to hire her. I can hobble along with Gail for a while longer. So I say, "Well, Michael, it's your call, but Hillary is not the ideal candidate for me. I caution you to make sure she is right for your organization before you make the decision to hire her. Thanks for your feedback, and I'll contact Human Resources to continue the recruiting process."

John, the proverbial suck-up, comments as he's leaving my office, "Wise decision, Boss. That girl was not the right fit." I just give him a nod, though I should add, *She's not a girl! She's a grown woman.* But those words would be wasted on a jerk like John. I also don't care enough to correct him.

I must call Human Resources and let them know my disappointment with their candidate selection. I'll ask Jim Waters to take over the recruitment process from Glenn. Jim shares my conservative views and doesn't get caught up in the affirmative action, diversity, and political correctness stuff that keeps me from specifying and getting the exact characteristics I want in my assistant. Those HR folks have too much power. I've got to start making the same demands as Anthony Fonetti. His mantra is "I control my department and my hiring, not HR." He gets to hire anybody he wants. He just hired one of his good friends, and both his son and his daughter are working for Sanger. You will never, ever see a person of color in his organization. He barely hires women unless they're related or have some other personal connection to him.

I dial Jim's number to get the ball rolling. "Hey, Jim, I need your help. The candidate HR brought in for an interview today was a huge mistake. I thought I've been quite clear about the qualifications I want, but apparently no one in that department is listening. Will you take over the recruitment process for this position?" Jim agrees and said he'll get back to me to discuss it further.

Michael can have Hillary, and I hope he lives to regret bringing her into his department. He'd better not come whining to me when she turns out to be a major disappointment. These liberals are always spouting off about giving women and people of color a chance. I'm not willing to lower my standards to bring in people who lack the qualifications and polish necessary to work for me. I had to go through years of studying until I was ready to drop. I spent hours late into the night to learn everything possible about my job to achieve the level I'm at today. No way am I going to bring in a Black woman who was laid off from her job because of poor performance. She will not come here and embarrass me with her ghetto ways and nappy hair. No way! She said her layoff was due to cost-cutting measures, but they probably kicked her out the door because of poor performance. I don't blame them. She deserved to be laid off if she wasn't performing at the level required for the position.

It all goes back to HR for hiring her in the first place. They're always trying to meet those affirmative action quotas by bringing in deadweights. I'm glad we have Justices John Roberts, Anthony Scalia, and Clarence Thomas on the Supreme Court to vote against affirmative action. Justice Thomas is a great example of an accomplished Black man who doesn't compromise his principles to support preferential treatment for any group. Oh well—tomorrow's another day. I know Jim will come through for me.

3 HILLARY

Another Day of Disappointment!

I had such high hopes of working at Sanger with Lucia. Little did I know the disappointments awaiting me when I walked into the amazingly decorated Sanger lobby. The first person to greet me was a guy from Human Resources named Glenn Hendricks. For some reason, I felt an immediate connection with him. Given the manner in which I was treated during my layoff, I totally lost confidence in HR. I hated to be talked at like I had no feelings and was just another notch in the layoff belt. Glenn seemed so different, with genuineness in his words and tone, that he made me feel welcome without coming across as being scripted.

"Hillary Montgomery, welcome to Sanger," he said. "I'm so glad you're here. It's a pleasure to meet you. My office is right around the corner." As we entered his modest office, he was again very welcoming. "Please come in and have a seat. May I get you some water?"

Once we settled into Glenn's office, he offered

words of assurance. "We haven't had a candidate with your skills and competencies since we announced this position. I'm very impressed with your fluency in Spanish. There isn't a need for it in this position, but I applaud bilingual professionals like you."

I blushed. "Thanks, Glenn; it's a language I love."

"Hillary, you have a full day of interviews, including one panel interview, but you'll do fine." He gave me a heads-up about the people who would be interviewing me. "John Griffin can have an intimidating style, but ignore his rough demeanor. He's a brilliant professional but is very tough on all candidates. You'll love Michael Dunlap. He's a great guy and a gentle giant who also knows his stuff. The executive assistant position reports to a vice president by the name of Darryl Kelsey. He's supersharp and is by far the toughest interviewer." Glenn told me Michael Dunlap and John Griffin were on a first-name basis. However, he emphasized, "I know I don't have to tell you this, but do not, under any circumstances, refer to Darryl Kelsey as anything other than 'Mr. Kelsey.'" Glenn reiterated that I was a perfect fit for the position and said, "Go into all of the interviews with the confidence your experience brings to the role. You'll do just fine."

I first met with Michael Dunlap, and he was exactly as Glenn had described. I immediately felt comfortable with him. When I shook his hand, he smiled and said, "Welcome, Hillary."

I responded. "Thank you, Mr. Dunlap."

"Please, call me Michael." He offered me a seat at his conference table and didn't assume the normal position of authority at his desk, with me sitting at a distance across from him, but sat next to me and made continuous, smiling eye contact.

"I am very impressed with your background, Hillary. You have excellent skills and a college degree. What led you to apply for the position at Sanger?"

I knew I'd be asked this question, so I gave the answer I had rehearsed numerous times. "I had a wonderful two years with my former company but unfortunately was laid off because of budget reductions." I was hesitant to mention the layoff, but I believe that honesty pays and knew he would find out anyway.

Michael's response was most encouraging: "Hey, in today's volatile economic environment, layoffs happen to the best of us." He then asked several questions, including "Where do you want to go with your professional career?" and "What's your ultimate career goal?" No one had ever cared enough to ask me about my career goals on other job interviews.

"I want to utilize the knowledge and skills from my degree to attain a meaningful and challenging position in Information Systems. I love working with computers. The icing on the cake would be a position that also utilized my bilingual skills. I'm fluent in Spanish."

Michael's face showed his surprise as he said, "Wow! I'm impressed. I think being bilingual is one of the best assets a professional can bring into an international company, given our global customers. I believe we lost a client last year because we lacked that kind of diversity."

I left Michael's office feeling great about the interview, which felt more like an ordinary conversation. What a likable guy!

Next, I met with the Information Systems team. I think most of them were in their twenties; a couple might even have been in their teens. They asked lots of questions about my academic background and also presented a few problems for me to solve. I was able to breeze through the problems and got a couple of high fives. They took me to lunch afterward and shared what they liked about working for Sanger. I was pleased and surprised when the team said they were pulling for me to get the job—especially because I could tell they were being sincere.

At one o'clock, I met with John Griffin. He made no effort to hide his disappointment when I entered the room. He actually frowned when I walked in. I'm not one to pull the race card, but I believe he was surprised to see a Black woman walk into his office. I've encountered racist stares before, and his was on par with the worst I've ever received. His greeting was equally disappointing. Unlike Michael Dunlap, he sat at his large desk and, without getting up, motioned for me to sit in a chair across from him. It was clear he wanted as much space as possible between us.

His first question was very direct: "Ms. Montgomery, why are you interviewing for an administrative position with Sanger when you have a college degree?"

I took a deep breath and explained, "This position will make full use of my diverse skills and give me the opportunity to work on other challenging projects described in the job announcement. I see an opportunity to grow from this experience and hopefully to gain access to other opportunities in the future."

He then threw a bombshell. "Ms. Montgomery, you have a college degree, but I'm not familiar with the university you attended. Was this an online degree program?" He had the audacity to say, before I could respond, "We at Sanger are cautious about online degrees because many are from suspect diploma mills for people who can't make it in our reputable higher-education institutions."

I was furious but maintained my composure. "No, sir, I attended a four-year academic institution, Meyers University, and graduated with honors."

The racist creep responded, "Oh, I see. Is that one of those historically Negro colleges? Jerome in the mailroom went to one of those colleges."

I bit my lip as I responded. "Meyers University is one of the top schools in Alabama and is also nationally ranked. I'm surprised you haven't heard of it."

He nodded nonchalantly. "Well, good for you. Of course, I'm just acting in the best interest of Sanger, which is why I asked."

He made a few other irrelevant inquiries and then said, "I know you're meeting with Mr. Kelsey next, and I don't want you to be late. Do you have any questions?" He never got up from his chair during the entire interview—or shall I say interrogation?

"No, sir. Thank you very much for your time."

"You're welcome. My assistant will take you up to Mr. Kelsey's office." He told his assistant on the intercom he was finished with our interview. I couldn't wait to get out of his office, and he obviously couldn't wait for me to leave. I didn't look back at him as his assistant ushered me out the door.

My last interview was with Mr. Darryl Kelsey. His assistant, Gail, met me at the elevator. She informed me she was his temporary assistant. As she sized me up from head to toe, she reminded me, "Mr. Kelsey"—she emphasized the "Mr."—"is extremely selective about who works in his organization. He has very high standards." As we reached his suite, she informed Mr. Kelsey over the intercom that I had arrived. I heard a strong bass voice say, "Yes, please bring her in."

Gail ushered me into his office, offered me water, and left, closing the door behind her. The disappointment John Griffin displayed when I walked into his office was no match for what I saw on Mr. Kelsey's face. He, too, couldn't hide his frown. What was with these Sanger executives? He also looked me up and down and then asked me to have a seat across from his desk, which was larger than John Griffin's.

After I sat, he started in: "Ms. Montgomery, tell me what led you to Sanger."

I gave him the same response I'd provided during the earlier interviews. I dared not mention I was here because of my best friend, Lucia. Lucia had made it clear I was not to let anyone know she is my friend. She filed a complaint against her former supervisor early last year and thought any mention of her name might spoil my chances of getting hired. I thank God for Lucia. She's always got my back.

After other typical interviewer questions, Mr. Kelsey focused on my recent layoff. "Ms. Montgomery, tell me about your last job and why you left that position." I could tell he was totally turned off with my being there, because he spoke his words robotically. He even stifled a yawn during his questioning.

The sad thing was, I was really hopeful when I first walked into his office and saw that he was a Black male. I even uttered thanks to God for answering my prayer. I should have waited. Instead, my prayer should have been *Help me, Lord, and deliver me from the prince of evil, whose office I just entered.* This guy had specific expectations of his assistant, and I clearly didn't meet them.

When I explained why I had been laid off, he looked at me in a manner that communicated how much he questioned the veracity of my explanation. I believe he wanted to say, *Yeah, do you really think I believe that, you liar?* Instead, he sarcastically uttered, "I see—cost-reduction measures. Humph." The sarcasm in his voice spoke volumes.

I felt the need to set the record straight, but my words fell on deaf ears when I said, "Sir, my supervisor praised my job performance, and I was being considered for a promotion before the layoffs."

Again he reacted coldly; then he cut me off to send a clear signal that nothing else I had to say mattered. "Yeah, I'm sure you were well regarded."

Like John Griffin, he also commented, "I don't understand why someone equipped with a college degree is interested in an executive assistant position. Explain this to me."

My response hung in the air like an ominous, dark cloud before a thunderstorm. "I am willing to take a lesser position to demonstrate my skills and strong work ethic, which I hope will lead to a position more aligned with my academic background."

Again, a distant nod. "I see. Well, I appreciate your interest in this position, and someone from HR will get back to you soon."

He then called Gail on the intercom to take me back to Human Resources. I was waiting to hear him yell out, "Gail, please get her out of my office, and hurry!" As Gail walked me back to HR, we ran into Glenn on the way to his office. She flippantly said, "Good luck," flashed me a contrived smile to overshadow her frown, and turned to go back to Mr. Kelsey's domain.

Glenn appeared happy to see me and asked how I felt about the interviews. I tried to act optimistic and hold back the tears on the verge of overflowing. "I think everything went well. You never know how things will turn out, but one can only hope for the best."

Glenn must have detected my disappointment, because he said, "Hillary, you are the most impressive candidate we've had for this role. To be honest, that applies to several other positions, too. I'm sure everything went well. You should hear back from me tomorrow. We have an urgent need to fill this position."

I could have hugged him for his encouragement after the disappointing interviews I'd just had with

John Griffin and Mr. Darryl Kelsey. "Thank you, Glenn. I really appreciate the encouragement and kindness you've shown me." We shook hands and I left. I'm almost positive I got a glimpse of Lucia as I left the lobby, but I didn't dare look in her direction, for fear our eyes might betray our secret.

When I got to my car, I couldn't hold back the tears any longer; I sat with my hands gripping the steering wheel and wept. I knew I wouldn't be offered the job. Glenn's positivity about my being a perfect fit was heartwarming, but he wasn't making the final decision.

It was hard to fathom having been subjected to such demeaning and insensitive treatment by leaders of a company with a huge sign in the lobby that read: WE TREAT OUR PEOPLE WITH DIGNITY AND RESPECT. This just wasn't fair! "Lord, did you hear me at all this morning? You said you'd never leave me or forsake me, but I didn't feel your presence when I met with John Griffin or Mr. Darryl Kelsey."

Mother would be upset that my professional, crisp white blouse was now smeared with mascara from my tears. I had been so sure today was the day. As hard as I tried, I had difficulty understanding and dealing with the treatment I had just experienced. To think a Black man in such an important role would toss me out like a piece of garbage....I wasn't asking either of those men for preferential treatment. All I wanted was fairness and respect.

They both acted as if my education and my work experience were fallacious. The audacity of John Griffin to infer my degree was from a diploma mill! I bet he didn't graduate magna cum laude. What an insensitive jerk! He apparently thinks Blacks receive degrees only from what he calls "historically Negro colleges."

Right now I feel like giving up, but I know that's not an option. It will be difficult, but I'm going to remain hopeful and trust God to take control of this situation.

4 DARRYL

Driving While Black Is Hazardous to Your Health

After a tough day at work, I'm enjoying driving to my gym on a crisp, rainy evening. I love the sound of rain and seeing the drops dance to different beats across my windshield. I shouldn't have had my car detailed yesterday. It's a sure thing that rain typically follows a car wash. My vehicle is always as immaculate as my personal appearance. I love the smell of a freshly washed car with that new-leather fragrance. I can see other drivers glancing over to check out my fine Mercedes, even in the rain. If only they could peer inside and see the fine, handsomely dressed gentleman behind the wheel. "Don't hate; imitate!" That's what Jerome, Sanger's ghetto mailroom guy, says. I, Mr. Darryl Kelsey, deserve the finer things in life, and that's what I'm always going to have.

I was confident today was the day the perfect assistant would walk through my door. Instead, I ended up having to deal with a nappy-headed sister.

I know Jim will get me the right person now that I'm no longer dealing with Glenn "Let's Do the Right Thing" Hendricks. Glenn had the audacity to try and push Hillary on me. He crowed about how qualified she was, and her degree was gravy, given the major project requirements. Who is he kidding? The signs are all there. Hillary Montgomery is not the right person to become my assistant. Jim assured me he has a great candidate coming in next Friday who will make up for the past candidate blunders.

I take much pride in my accomplishment of climbing the corporate ladder and achieving the vice president level. The good thing is, there are many more opportunities for further career growth. I can't wait to go to my high school reunion next month so I can strut my stuff.

Daffy Black Darryl—that's what they called me during high school. I was dark-skinned, overweight, and clumsy. I couldn't have gotten a date even if I'd paid a girl to go out with me. They laughed at me behind my back and to my face.

Charles Watson was the one who always picked on me and got others to join him. He was the bully of all bullies, and relentless in pointing out my every flaw—from my dark complexion to my hand-me-down clothes—especially when there was a crowd. No one in my class stood up for me, not a soul. One of the most hurtful moments was when they joked and laughed about my father's working as a garbage man. Charles made up rhymes about us. "Darryl, Darryl, he's our man, Daddy feeds him from the garbage can." "Big Black Darryl, he's so fat. That's what happens when you eat fried rat."

I hated Charles with a passion back then and still do today. I often daydreamed of beating him to a pulp. He was the most handsome guy on campus, the light-skinned athlete with the good hair, and I was the fat, dark-skinned, kinky-haired nerd whose daddy rode the trash truck. The girls flocked to him because of his light complexion and dark, wavy hair. Charles got lots of laughs at my expense, but we'll see who has the last laugh.

My father was a good man who worked his tail off to feed his seven kids. He worked any side job he could find. He literally worked himself to death because he wanted my mother to stay at home with us kids. She was his rock. They had true love and were always happy in spite of their circumstances. Daddy died of pneumonia at the age of fifty-two. He waited too long to get medical treatment. I was in my second year of college at the time and couldn't afford to go home for the funeral.

I still feel a strong sense of guilt to this day for not being there for my mother after Daddy died. A year later, she died of a broken heart. She was a sweet, strong woman and a true nurturer who could stretch a chicken ten different ways. After all, she had to feed seven hungry kids. I don't recall going to bed with a full stomach, but we certainly weren't starving.

Mama was the strict one, who drilled into our heads that we always had to be better than everyone else. She always said, "Black children have to be two hundred percent better to compete with white kids, and even that might not be enough. Don't ever settle for one hundred percent." She didn't mean we were less than white kids by this mandate. She meant we had to work twice as hard to receive proper recognition and similar achievements. She wasn't well educated, and she didn't spare the rod if we came home with anything less than a B. I was always proud to bring home my straight-A report cards. Those A's really made Mama happy; Daddy, too.

Daddy didn't have much education, either, but he valued it for his children. We all did well in school because of our parents' expectations of nothing less. Daddy used to tell me all the time, "Boy, you're somebody special in this world. Don't let the bad things people say to you get you down; you just keep on pushing. I can see great things happening for you one day. Don't you dare give up. I know the kids pick on you and how it hurts you, but you are a winner! *You are a winner!*" He's the reason I completely immersed myself in schoolwork. It became my primary outlet and motivated me always to attain good grades. My father's words impact me to this day. They come to me when I'm down or feel undue pressure on the job.

The church Daddy and Mama attended and loved had to raise funds to bury them both. I have never been a churchgoer. Jesus never did a thing for me when I was tormented all those years. If there is a God, He never brought anything but pain into my life. My parents told me to pray about the ridicule I suffered in high school, so I prayed and I prayed. But God never showed up, so I gave up on Him. I recall praying Charles would develop a disease that ruined his handsome face; then I went even further and prayed for his death.

Yet Charles became only more popular and more degrading in his conduct toward me. One of his dirtiest tricks was during the latter part of my senior year, when everyone was excited about the senior prom. I felt so dejected knowing none of the girls would dare go to the prom with me. Conniving Charles had a very cute girl, Sally Brown, ask me to be her date. I remember her saying, "Darryl, I want you to know I'm not like the rest of the kids. I like you and would be honored if you took me to the prom."

I couldn't believe my ears and was overwhelmed with joy. I never dreamed that Sally Brown would be interested in me. This was the happiest time of my entire high school experience—no, my entire life. I told my mom, and she was thrilled and began thinking about how they could manage to rent me a tuxedo for the night.

Then my happiness came to an abrupt end. I saw Sally with her friends in the cafeteria shortly before the prom one day when she didn't know I was behind her. She was laughing as she told them, "Can you believe Daffy Darryl thinks I'm really going to let him take me to the prom? Charles promised he'd take me out if I told Darryl I liked him. That silly fool believed me." Her friends were trying to get her attention and warn her that I was standing behind her, but she was having too much fun at my expense to catch on to their signals. I was devastated and turned and quickly walked away, ready to kill both Charles and Sally.

I cried a river of tears when I got home, and my mother tried to console me when I told her what had happened. She hugged me tightly while saying, "God loves you, and those two will get their due. You mark my words."

That's when I said, "God doesn't love me. How could He torment me this way? What kind of love is that? No—today and forever, there is no more God in my life."

I still think often about my parents' faith in God. They died with nothing, yet they were true believers, never did a bad deed to anyone. They were always willing to give generously out of their poverty. Daddy died just trying to survive. I never understood their joy. What did they have to praise God about—seven hungry mouths to barely feed and clothe? I still don't get it. Yet they loved Him with all their being. One day I asked my father, "Daddy, Why do you love God so much, when your life is such a struggle? We're so poor, and people look down on us."

I'll never forget his response. "Boy, I love God because He's my everything. I know I may have trials on this earth, but I look forward to the good time your mama and I will have when we meet God in heaven."

I couldn't comprehend his response. I responded, "Why can't you have some good times on Earth? Why do you have to wait until you die? Why doesn't God show His love for you now?"

Daddy looked at me with surprise and disappointment. "Why do you think God doesn't show me His love now? I have many good times on Earth today, right now. I may not be rich in material things, but I have the most wonderful woman on Earth, who loves me and her children unconditionally. I have seven wonderful children, and none of them gives us any trouble. I have a loving church family who supports us in every way. I have a steady job when so many others are unemployed." Daddy's faith was unshakable, and I knew nothing I said would ever cause it to waver. I quit asking him questions about God after coming to that realization.

I had the most expensive granite headstones put on my parents' graves after I started making decent money at Sanger. My siblings contributed some. Although they're doing well, they're not in my league financially. They didn't commit to the rigor I demonstrated as a student. They were good students, but I was exceptional. I excelled in every subject in high school and won a full, four-year academic scholarship to college. The scholarship didn't cover my food, so I often struggled to have enough to eat and do well in my studies. I lived from Pell Grant to Pell Grant, eating lots of ramen noodles. That's probably how I lost my weight. I'm glad I made the decision to keep it off.

Just like in high school, I was a loner in college and maintained my focus on excelling in my studies, graduating summa cum laude with a degree in information systems. My academic discipline paid off in an internship at Sanger that led to a full-time position. Sanger recognized quality and hired me after I graduated from college. I now have my master's in information systems, thanks to Sanger's generous tuition reimbursement program. Life is truly good, and it's only because of my hard work. No one else helped me along the way. Maybe that's why I'm not a religious person. I'm not saying God

doesn't exist. He just didn't send any special blessings my way.

I am totally immersed in these thoughts of
the past when I see whirling lights in my rearview
window and hear a police car siren behind me. What
the hell is going on? Why am I being pulled over? I
know I'm not speeding, and everything works perfectly on my car. I pull over into a deserted parking
lot, and the police car follows. A tall, burly white
cop walks up to my car and barks, "Roll down your
window. I need to see your driver's license."

As I hand it to him, I ask why I was pulled over,
since I wasn't speeding. He doesn't answer and walks
back to his patrol car. When he comes back, he says,
"Get out of the car!"

Again, I ask why, and he answers, "I need you to
get out of the car, now! A car similar to this one was
involved in a robbery."

I respond as politely as possible, "Officer, I just
left my office and have several witnesses who can
immediately vouch for that."

The burly cop says, "Get out of the car, and I
mean now!" I get out of the car, and suddenly two
other police cars pull up.

Giant raindrops begin to pound my body,
and the burly cop tells me to walk over to an uncov-
ered area where a large puddle of water has formed.
He yells out, "Kneel there while we check you out."

I think about my Armani suit and my new Bally

loafers getting soaked. Why in God's name do I have to kneel in the mud? But I do as he says, and he handcuffs me tightly with those white plastic cuffs. He walks back to where the other cops have gathered in their rain gear, and they laugh about something—probably this Black man kneeling in a puddle of water in an expensive suit.

I'm getting totally soaked and surrounded by muddy water. My heart is racing. I think of the number of Black men who have been shot by police for the slightest movement, even while handcuffed, so I remain still, even as thoughts race through my head. *Am I going to die in this mud? Will the burly cop tell others the truth when they ask what happened to me? Will they plant narcotics on me to justify my arrest and tarnish my reputation? Will anyone believe my story? Once again, God has failed to come to my rescue.* Before I realize it, tears of anger and dread are forming as I become consumed with the utmost humiliation, rage, and powerlessness. I'm glad for the rain. I never want these cops to see a strong Black man of my caliber crying.

After about fifteen minutes, once I'm cold and shivering, the burly cop comes over to me and snaps, in the most demeaning manner, "You can stand now." He removes the handcuffs and smiles as he says, "Oh, sorry about this—your car was not involved in the robbery after all." The bastard then tells me, "Hey, I like your set of wheels. Bet it cost you a few bucks, right?" Before I get into the car, he adds with a smirk, "I'm sorry about your beautiful suit. I bet it cost a lot of money, too, huh? But what the hell—I'm sure you have a few more like it. Stay out of trouble, now. You hear?"

I can see the cops laughing as I drive away. There's a Black cop among them, and he's laughing right along with the others.

My tears are falling like mad now, so I drive straight home, instead of to the gym. By the time I get to my condo, my head is about to burst with rage. I literally weep as I remove my mud-soaked loafers, suit, shirt, tie, underwear, and socks and toss them all into a plastic garbage bag. Who do they think they are, treating me this way? They're supposed to protect all citizens, not humiliate those who have Black faces. Those guys think they have total power over men like me, but we'll see who has the most power. This Black man is not a weakling. Nobody messes with Darryl Kelsey, Mr. Darryl Kelsey.

I managed to get the burly cop's badge number and his car number as I was kneeling in the muddy puddle. I have a photographic memory, and the bastard will soon wish he had never pulled me over. Before I get into the shower, I write down all of his information in my little green book.

I feel somewhat better after I shower and change into comfortable clothes. The plastic bag filled with the reminders of my ordeal is staring at me, taunting me. I grab it and walk down to the Dumpster and throw the bag into it with all the force I can muster.

I will have the last word about this incident, you despicable jerk—just wait and see.

5 LUCIA

Some Things Just Don't Make Sense

"Lucia Hernandez, *niña, usted debe estar avergonzado de sí mismo!*"
Yes, I should be ashamed of myself. My best friend in the whole world interviewed for a job today, and I couldn't even acknowledge her. I told her to make sure she didn't in any way mention she knows me. I know she saw me as she left the lobby. Even though she was cool and avoided making eye contact with me, we are close like sisters and I could see a cloud hovering over her when she left the building. I know Darryl Kelsey, Señor Darryl Kelsey, the egotistical maniac, will not see Hillary as fit for his kingdom. She's not white and doesn't have long, blond hair.

I can't figure this guy out. He doesn't like Black women. Doesn't he know that's an insult to his own mother? Given his dark complexion, it's obvious she was Black. I don't get these Black guys who are always disrespecting their women. I think they don't like themselves and take it out on the very women who stand behind them through both good and bad times. Not me—I'd tell them to kiss the part of my behind that gets no sunlight.

For once, though, I was hoping fairness and integrity would prevail and the most competent person would get the position. So what if Hillary's complexion is mocha brown, she's slightly heavy, and her hair is in its natural, beautiful state? I often drift into this delusional state of mind, but then reality always hits me squarely in the face. I just pray the God Hillary serves and loves so much will honor her with a job at Sanger. She is truly a good Christian woman and loves everyone. I envy her positive outlook on life, considering the letdowns she's recently experienced.

Sanger is a great company, and, in spite of my trials, I'm glad I've been employed there for almost seven years. I have had to deal with tremendous marginalization because of my Spanish accent. One would think my accent would have improved after I've been in the States for over twenty years. I migrated here at the age of fifteen to join my parents after living with my aunt in Hermosillo, Mexico, while they were getting established in their new country. I could barely speak English when I arrived, but I mastered the language quickly, so it's been painful to stomach the letdowns when I've developed excellent presentations for our customers, only to have someone else present. I can still hear my supervisor saying, "Lucia, you're so talented, but your accent makes it difficult for customers to understand you. Please don't take it personally. You do excellent work, and we'll make sure you get full credit. We'll also explore getting you into one of those accent-reduction programs in the not-too-distant future."

It's always amazing to me how my white colleagues with strong Southern accents don't get the same treatment. It's a standing joke that most of us can hardly understand them at times, yet my leadership finds their accents to be most charming, while my Spanish accent is reason enough for my colleagues to present my work products and benefit from the important visibility needed to climb the corporate ladder.

Give me the credit? No way. My conniving supervisor, Sheryl Murray, usually acknowledges me as a last resort. She cleverly takes full credit for my work and keeps me in the background. There are exceptions, of course, such as when there's a Hispanic client. That's when Sheryl parades me around like the first-prize float in the Macy's Thanksgiving Day parade.

I filed a complaint against her last year because she reneged on a commitment she made to me when Sanger was pursuing a major contract with Castillo Information Systems. Sheryl was so convincing when she said, "Lucia, we have a very special client Sanger is pursuing. If you play a major role in landing this client, you'll be handsomely rewarded. Please know, however, as long as you're a major contributor, even if the deal falls through, you're next in line for a key promotion. The promotion will be effective at the beginning of the new fiscal year." I was naive enough to believe the lying witch.

Finally, the opportunity I'd longed for all those years had taken center stage. It was a dream come true, and success was no longer out of reach for the resident Latina with the heavy Spanish accent. I was determined to make the best of this project, even if I had to work eighty hours a week. My level of enthusiasm was off the Richter scale. I translated technical documents from Spanish to English and wrote key provisions of the proposal. There's no way they could have competed for the contract without my contributions. I was motivated by the fact that a promotion was imminent, with or without a successful Castillo contract award, and confident that my performance was above and beyond expectations and the promotion would be well deserved, based solely on my merit.

Sanger executives, including the unapproachable Mr. Darryl Kelsey, praised the quality of my work as we pursued the Castillo contract. They were equally amazed at how quickly I was able to get the job done. Sheryl had no choice but to give me credit for the vast amount of work I had accomplished. Everyone knew she didn't speak a word of

Spanish and it was I who translated all the contracts from English.

Sheryl reluctantly allowed me to make a presentation to the clients, albeit a minor role in the overall scheme of things. It was important to make sure the Spanish clients saw Sanger as a champion of diversity. Señorita Lucia Hernandez was the Spanish ornament hanging from the miniature Sanger diversity tree. I cringed whenever Sheryl, with a phony smile, said, "Lucia, we'd like for you to speak as much Spanish as possible during your presentation. It will be well received by our customer."

To add insult to injury, in addition to the contract translations, I had to tutor the vice president of marketing in basic Spanish. The useless assignment still sticks in my craw. Tutoring a highly paid executive while juggling a major project—what's up with that? It's mind-boggling that he didn't just purchase one of those Spanish immersion DVDs. It's not like Sanger didn't have the funds to cover it. In spite of my best efforts, his command of the most basic Spanish was abysmal. Thank goodness he decided not to attempt speaking the language during the Castillo contract review. The Castillo team would have laughed hysterically all the way back to Mexico.

Everyone was confident Sanger would land the Castillo contract, so it was a somber day when we learned that Castillo had awarded the contract to our competition. Although the Castillo team liked our proposal, they thought our competitor offered more incentives and lowered the cost of doing business. I was as disappointed as the Sanger executives, but I knew a promotion was imminent after my major contributions—until that snake, Sheryl, suddenly had major amnesia and offered the promotion to one of her protégés, a white male with less experience and less education.

Mortified doesn't come close to describing my feelings. I felt betrayed and used and, to put it in simple street language, pimped. I was a feisty young girl and had a quick temper that often got me into trouble, both at school and at home. My mother came up with what she thought was the perfect remedy for my short fuse. She taught me to count to one hundred before speaking when I was seething with anger. Well, one hundred didn't cut it in this case. I needed to count to one million before I could utter a single word. To make matters worse, Sheryl didn't have the professional courtesy to communicate her reasoning for denying me the promotion. She simply chose to ignore me, perhaps thinking I'd eventually get over my disappointment and put the whole thing behind me.

I decided not to sit back and let her get away with breaching an oral promise on which I had in good faith relied and expected her to follow through. I had hoped she might prove me wrong by demonstrating that she actually had a shred of integrity, but no such luck.

I filed a complaint with Jim Waters, my human resources specialist or, better yet, my human reprobate specialist. The spineless wonder went directly to Sheryl and told her about the complaint. He offered her a few tips on how to "appropriately" (wink, wink) deal with me. There are no secrets at Sanger, and Jim's antics got back to me through a colleague with whom Sheryl had shared Jim's instructions. He told Sheryl to tell me that I misinterpreted her words when we spoke about a promotion. She was to emphatically remind me that in no way had she promised me a promotion but had said that I would be *considered* for one. But Sheryl and I never had the conversation, because, as fate would have it, Jim had a family crisis and took personal leave for about a month. I believe divine intervention takes many forms.

Glenn Hendricks restored my faith in Human Resources when he took over Jim's projects, including my complaint. He consistently keeps the "human" in "human resources" and isn't a typical pawn for management. Even when he doesn't get the support he needs from them, no one tries harder to ensure fair treatment than he does.

When he discovered the shenanigans Jim and Sheryl had pulled, he halted my colleague's promotion and became relentless in pushing for the one I had been promised. In turn, Sheryl quickly placed the entire promotion idea on hold, cleverly citing cost-cutting measures as the rationale for her decision.

In the end, neither my colleague nor I was promoted. It was a bitter pill to swallow, but at least Glenn did all he could to help me. Ever since my complaint, Sheryl has been cool and barely communicates with me. She interacts just enough to give me assignments and avoid a retaliation complaint. I would love to go for her jugular, but I have claustrophobia and a prison cell won't work for me.

Sheryl did receive disciplinary action, a written warning, as a result of her promotion promise. The warning cited her lack of sound judgment in making a promotion commitment for a position that wasn't within her authority to approve. I was told Jim Waters shredded the disciplinary-action document the same day, at the request of John Griffin.

I cling to the hopeful words Hillary shares with me: "Don't worry, my sister—brighter days are ahead. You just wait and see. When God closes one door, rest assured he's already opening a better one." I believe her and wish my faith were as strong as hers. I rely more frequently on a saying from Hillary's grandmother when I think of the evils John and Jim have pulled off: "Every dog has its day, and really bad dogs have two days." If that holds true, Sheryl's two days are way overdue. Jim and John may have at least three or four coming. ¡*Aleluya!*

6 HILLARY

Hallelujah, My Time Has Come!

I hear the phone ringing. I'm still in a semisleep stupor, and my body is fighting the need to gain alertness. The call goes to the answering machine, and I hear the caller saying, "Hello, Hillary. This is Glenn Hendricks."

I'm immediately alert and grab the phone. "Hello, Glenn. How are you?"

"I'm fine, thank you. I'm calling to let you know you were not offered the position you interviewed for last week as the executive assistant for Mr. Darryl Kelsey."

My heart sinks. *Oh no, God, not again. This just can't keep happening to me.* It's been a week since my interview. I was hoping and praying that bad news wouldn't once again be on the horizon. What have I done to deserve this constant rejection?

I hear Glenn speaking. "Hillary, are you still there? The good news is, you have been selected for another position. I think you will like it much better. You remember Michael Dunlap? He has an

IT project analyst position opening he thinks is a perfect fit for your skills. He was impressed with you and wants you to start as soon as possible."

Now my heart is pounding and my tears start falling uncontrollably. I'm saying inside my head, *Thank you, Jesus! Thank you, Jesus!* My words come tumbling out, "Thank you, Glenn! Thank you so much."

In what I've quickly learned is true Glenn encouraging fashion, he responds, "Your skills were the real selling point for the position; my role was minimal. You'll have to go through the pre-employment screening process, including drug testing, before you start work." That's not a problem for me, because the only drug I take periodically is Motrin for menstrual cramps.

We agree I'll come in on Monday to complete the job application and the prescreening process. Glenn congratulates me and tells me how much he looks forward to having me on the Sanger team. I believe he's sincere, not merely speaking scripted HR jargon, like the HR folks on my last job.

I hang up and shout, "Hallelujah! Thank you, Jesus!" I am going to be employed, finally. I can keep my apartment with my own washer and dryer. Thank you, Lord! I drop to my knees in prayer and thank God for his grace and mercy. "I know I'm not deserving. Lord, thank you for this opportunity. Please forgive my doubt and my questioning your faithfulness. I promise to show the fruits of the spirit and love in all of my actions on this job. Amen."

I dial Lucia's cell to tell her the good news. I know she's at work, so I leave a message telling her to call me back—it's important! Then I send her a text to call me at her earliest convenience. She will be thrilled to learn that we will both be working for the same company.

I start dialing my mother's number but decide to wait until every "i" is dotted and every "t" crossed before I call her. Mother means well, but she will think of everything I need to do right away to prepare for work. I want to experience this time with uninterrupted joy, something I haven't felt for some time. I think about my mother's continuous prayers for me and her team of "prayer warriors." Those women can pray the stars out of a clear night's sky.

I'm sure those prayers opened this door for me and decide I'd better call Mother after all, to share the good news. She doesn't pick up, so I leave a voice mail: "Hi Mom, you'll be happy to know your sweet daughter was offered a position with Sanger International. It's even better than the position I originally interviewed for. Thank you and your prayer warriors for lifting me up. I know your prayers made the difference. I love you, and we'll talk later."

The phone rings, and Lucia's caller ID pops up.

I answer and try to sound very sad as I say, "Hey, girl, Glenn called to let me know I didn't get the position working for Mr. Darryl Kelsey. I wasn't a fit with Mr. Kelsey's expectations, and they're continuing their search."

Lucia takes a deep breath and says, "I don't believe this crap. Who in the hell does he think he is? You are more than qualified for the position. You're a computer whiz, you have a degree, you're supersmart. What more do they want? I'm so sorry, Hillary. You deserve better, and this really pisses me off."

I can't hold it in any longer, so, with the utmost jubilation, I say, "My sister, I got a better position, with Michael Dunlap as an IT project analyst."

Lucia screams, "¡*Aleluya!* ¡*Aleluya!* Girl, you're going to give me a heart attack. I am so happy for you! We have to celebrate tonight. Make dinner reservations wherever you want to go, and it's on me."

My mother's thoughts creep into my head, and I say, "Let's wait until after my first week on the job."

Lucia picks up on this hesitation and immediately chides me. "Listen, girlfriend, we are going to celebrate *tonight*! I know you too well, so stop those Mother Montgomery anxious thoughts right now. You are going to get through all of the prescreening with flying colors. Today is a new day for you, so no looking back and no bad thoughts. You hear me?" I answer yes, and her words actually reignite my enthusiasm. Lucia excitedly responds, "Dinner it is, and I know you like the Italian restaurant on Palm Street. I'll make reservations and meet you there at seven o'clock sharp. I am so happy for you. I can't believe we're going to be working for the same company. How cool is that!"

After we say good-bye, I can't stop smiling. To think I allowed doubt to consume me, when the right job was mine all along. I thank God for His faithfulness. Now it's time for rejoicing with my main man, James Brown, and my favorite song, "There Was a Time." I dance until I break into what James Brown called a "cold sweat."

7 DARRYL

They Finally Got It Right!

I t's 10:45 a.m., and Jim had better make sure I have the right woman for my assistant position today, not tomorrow. I've waited long enough. He promised she'd be here by last Friday, almost a week ago. No one plays Darryl Kelsey, and Jim knows that better than anyone. I phone him to make sure she's coming for the eleven o'clock interview. Jim answers and, knowing why I'm calling, says, "The candidate is already here and will be on time."

He puts up a good front when we're on the phone, but Jim knows what I want. It cracks me up when he says, in his most formal tone, "Mr. Kelsey, you know Sanger is committed to a fair and equitable hiring process. I know you want the candidate of your preference, but please understand we select candidates based on their skills and abilities, and not other, irrelevant attributes." Jim assures me offline that he says this in case anyone else is listening around him. Unlike we vice presidents, Jim and others of his classification work in cubicles.

It's almost 10:55 now, and I wonder what she looks like. My vision of the perfect candidate has changed a bit from my original version. Now I imagine her being about five feet, six inches tall, with emerald-green eyes. She's not too skinny but has a slightly slim build. She holds my status and my position in the highest regard. Yes, that's what I want—not some nappy-headed, heavy sister who will act as if she's the boss and won't respect my authority.

I've been through put-downs from sisters like Hillary at my high school, but never again. They always laughed when Charles made fun of me. There's no way women like that will be part of Mr. Darryl Kelsey's staff. Let Michael Dunlap hire those laid-off sisters with no talent, but not Mr. Darryl Kelsey. Michael will soon come to me, whining about how he made a mistake in hiring Hillary. I'll show him no sympathy whatsoever. He's such a wimp, like the rest of those "let's do the right thing" liberals.

Gail knocks on my door. Instead of using the intercom, she pokes her head in and says, "Mr. Kelsey, the candidate, Cathy Fisher, has arrived for her interview." As I rise to greet Cathy, an angel from heaven walks into the room. Jim has definitely hit a home run this time. Cathy has an hourglass figure, a smile that would melt the butter on my pancakes, and the most beautiful blue eyes.

So what if they're not emerald green? I'm equally fond of blue. She has flowing blond hair, the color of honey, not the fake weaves and extensions the sisters are wearing these days. We shake hands, and hers are soft and warm, like she's been wearing those paraffin mittens they use to soften hands at the nail shop near my condo. She looks into my eyes as she says, "Mr. Kelsey, thanks for taking the time out of your busy schedule to interview me today."

I can see pure admiration as she steals a glance around my office. I offer her a chair at my table and sit next to her. She crosses those beautiful long legs as she sits, adjusting her skirt in the most ladylike but alluring manner.

Cathy hands me her resume to review, but Jim has already given me an advance copy. As I ask my typical questions about the requisite skills, she answers in the most polished manner. She doesn't have Hillary's technical skills, but who cares? She exceeds my expectations for the type of woman I want as my assistant. I ask what led her to Sanger.

"Mr. Kelsey, my position was eliminated during cost-cutting measures. I was not the most tenured and experienced, so I was let go."

Unlike I did with Hillary, I offer Cathy words of assurance. "Don't worry—these things happen to the best of us. It certainly won't have a bearing on your consideration for this position."

Cathy smiles. "Thanks, Mr. Kelsey. I've had several rejections since I was laid off." It's not a problem for me that her previous company let her go. It's a plus, in fact. I'm sure a company had to be desperate to lay off a woman of this caliber. Cathy further explains, "I recently relocated to Arkansas from California. I'm glad I made the move, although the South takes a little getting used to."

I notice she has three tiny earrings in each ear. It would normally bother me for a woman to wear too many earrings to an interview, but not Cathy. I don't waste more time asking meaningless questions and jump to the main point: "Cathy, you're certainly the candidate who not only meets but exceeds my expectations. When can you start work?"

Cathy responds, "Oh, thank you, Mr. Kelsey. I will need a couple of weeks before starting full-time to tie up some loose ends, but I could start earlier, on a part-time basis, if needed."

That's perfect; it will allow Cathy to spend some time with Gail before she begins full-time. I will ask Jim to expedite her start date.

"Cathy, thank you for your interest in Sanger and the executive assistant position. I'm confident we'll make a great team." She agrees as she uncrosses those beautiful legs and stands to shake my hand. I explain, while still holding her hand, "HR will make the formal offer, but you are definitely the right person for the job." I buzz Gail, and then the angel leaves my office.

I'm smiling widely as I dial Jim's extension. "You hit a home run, my friend. Please proceed with hiring Cathy right away. She's a knockout, and I owe you lunch."

Of course, Jim goes into formal, blah-blah-blah HR-speak: "Mr. Kelsey, you know lunch is not necessary and Cathy was the next candidate on the short list. As I've reminded you on multiple occasions, we will follow company protocol and ensure Cathy goes through proper prescreening of references and a background check before we commit to officially hiring her." Jim expresses some hesitation about initially bringing Cathy on part-time, but I tell him to make it happen. When I see him away from his cubicle, I know we'll have a big laugh about this phone call and we'll definitely do lunch.

I look out on the beautiful, sunny day from my floor-to-ceiling office windows. My colleagues will envy me even more when Cathy shows up as my new executive assistant. The old hags they have can't compete with her. Yes, Cathy is just the right woman to assist Mr. Darryl Kelsey.

Wouldn't it be something if I walked into my high school reunion with her? Heads would spin like the girl's in *The Exorcist*. All the brothers walk a little taller with a pretty white woman on their arm, especially a blonde. The sisters would be mad as hell, though. I would do cartwheels if Sally Brown saw me with a beauty like Cathy. We'll cross that bridge when we get to it. Let me first get Cathy hired. If there is a God, He has finally taken notice of me on this day.

8 HILLARY

I Love My New Job!

I completed the prescreening process with no difficulty, just as Lucia said. Thank you, Jesus—I am now a Sanger employee. It's been three weeks on the job, and I love my new position. I'm using computer algorithms and problem-solving methods that my team deeply needed. My computer skills have proven to be invaluable in getting projects that have fallen behind back on schedule. Michael was right when he said my skill set was a perfect fit for this position. His warm demeanor makes him a nice guy to work for; he greets everyone daily with a smile and makes us feel welcome and valued, though don't get me wrong—it's clear he has no use for slackers and holds people accountable. I love the whole team I'm working with and appreciate their brilliant minds, so eager to make a positive impact. I am blessed to be part of this group and pray I will have a long-term career at this company.

Glenn Hendricks is off the chain with his support. He's checked on me once each week and offered his assistance for anything I might need. He's restored my faith in HR, and I can't thank him enough for his advocacy and his genuine kindness. I've heard office gossip going around about his being gay and maybe even having an affair with Michael. It's amazing how office gossip, especially when there's sex involved, spreads like California wildfires. It makes no difference if the veracity of the stories is questionable. Both Michael and Glenn are awesome people, and who in the world cares if they're gay? I appreciate the fact that they're real, not like some of the phonies Lucia has told me to avoid.

One thing's for sure: everyone shudders when the name Darryl Kelsey is mentioned. Whenever anyone calls him "Darryl Kelsey," someone else says mockingly, "No, you must say '*Mr.* Darryl Kelsey.'" Although I usually jump to defend my Black brothers, I don't have that impulse with Mr. Darryl Kelsey. I ran into him in Starbucks on the second floor one day and made the mistake of saying hello. He looked at me as if I were a turd in a punch bowl and gave me a weak nod, without making eye contact. He's the most insecure and conceited man I've ever encountered, someone with real issues who's in desperate need of on-the-couch professional counseling. He struts around with his nose in the air like he's on a Versace runway in Paris or has just been crowned the King of England.

Still, as much as I hate to admit it, there's something beyond my comprehension that touches me about Darryl. God knows the brother looks handsome in his fine, tailored suits and perfectly matching accessories—from the shirt and tie to the spit-shined shoes. Nothing, and I mean absolutely nothing, can beat a Black man's swagger. I get giddy every time I see President Obama walking to board *Air Force One*. Mr. President has a mean swagger; it's probably one of the reasons so many Republican males hate him. They just can't give our president a break. I'm not in any way comparing Darryl to President Obama, though; it's only the strut that they have in common.

Darryl's ego (I refer to him as Darryl only when he's in my thoughts) has gotten even more inflated since the new blonde, Cathy, was hired as his assistant. It's the talk of the building how the HR piranha Jim Waters made sure he recruited an assistant that fits every one of Darryl's expectations. The word on the street is, she may be pretty but doesn't have anywhere near the skills I brought to the table. That's okay; God knew the right position for me. I couldn't be happier working with Michael and his team.

As fate would have it, I run into Cathy when entering the ladies' room this morning and she flashes a smile, showing her brilliant white teeth. No doubt about it—the girl is beautiful. She introduces herself. "Hi, I'm Cathy Fisher, the new executive assistant to Mr. Darryl Kelsey."

I tell her I'm also new and congratulate her on joining Sanger. We chat briefly, about which department I report to and her elation at being Mr. Kelsey's assistant. Cathy is a real talker and also shares, "I'm trying to adjust quickly to my new role, but there's so much to learn because my skills are a bit rusty. My Kelsey is so patient with me. He is such a gem to work with."

I cringe inside at her comments. My skills are sharp but not good enough to be hired by a Black man who pays more attention to physical characteristics. I'd like to know why he has this apparent loathing for Black women. It's not Cathy's fault, though, so I don't have any ill will toward her. I actually find her quite friendly, so I decide I'll treat her with respect.

Cathy seems genuinely pleased to connect with another new person; in fact, she says, "Hillary, I'd love it if we could do lunch soon and get to know each other better. There are some neat restaurants nearby, or we can just go to the Sanger cafeteria."

"Yes," I say, "I'd love to join you for lunch after I settle in with my team and fully grasp my new responsibilities."

We use the toilet, wash up, and are on our way.

I run into Glenn on the way back to my cubicle and, after thanking him once again, give him a big hug. I immediately apologize and tease him, "Sorry, Glenn—I got carried away and didn't mean to hug you. I don't want a sexual harassment complaint during my first month on the job."

He laughs and says, "Don't worry, sexual harassment is unwanted behavior and your hug was definitely wanted." Then, with a slightly sad look, he adds, "Hillary, in my role, a hug is almost unheard of. I'm so happy you're with Sanger."

As we continue on to our respective destinations, I think about how much I like Glenn. I hope I can take him to lunch or dinner after a few months and get to know him better. Listen to me—I'm already talking in terms of months later. I feel great about my newfound confidence and offer up a silent prayer: *Thank you, God, for looking after me.*

9 LUCIA

Best Friends Forever

It's been great having Hillary join Sanger and get the opportunity to show off her many talents. I overheard a member of Michael's team telling Michael how grateful he is Hillary wasn't selected as Mr. Kelsey's assistant. He was raving about her IT skills. He also said her overall positive attitude has given the team a much-needed lift. I had to refrain from shouting out, "¡*Esta es mi muchacha!*" ("That's my girl!") Hillary and I have agreed to keep our sisterhood on the down-low, at least until we feel totally secure about the environment. As women of color, unlike our white male and female counterparts, we are often viewed suspiciously when we have close relationships at work. God forbid we bring another woman of color into the work environment—it's as if we're plotting to launch some evil plan. So we act like casual acquaintances who've connected solely through Sanger pathways to avoid any unnecessary scrutiny. Hillary has always said I have a sixth sense. Don't ask me why, but I believe keeping our relationship to ourselves will pay off in the future.

Fate truly brought Hillary and me together. We were in the same computer class in college. The girl has a special love and mastery of computers like Oscar De La Hoya has a love and mastery of boxing. Our professor recognized her talent and showered her with praise. On the contrary, computers and I didn't get along at the time. I was terrible in the class and in danger of failing. I went to the professor's office and asked if I could get an extra-credit assignment or anything to boost my grade and avoid flunking the class. He was totally unsympathetic and said, "Miss Hernandez, you need to get your head on straight and get with it in class. You're not putting forth the effort; therefore, I will not assign you extra credit."

Hillary happened to be standing outside the open office door and heard my conversation with the professor. When I stepped out of his office, her words warmed my heart: "I apologize for eavesdropping, but if you're interested in tutoring assistance, I'm willing to work with you. I tutor a few other students, and it's no problem adding you if you're willing to pay a small hourly fee." Hell yes—I would have paid her $50 an hour to help me graduate on time, and she was asking for only $10 an hour. I shared with Hillary the problems I was having with my English class, and she offered to tutor me in that subject as well.

Not only does Hillary have computer savvy, she is an awesome teacher. She was so patient and helped me approach both classes in a new light. She could break down software algorithms to a level my brother's six-year-old son could grasp. I went from a low D in my computer class to a high C in only six weeks. If the class had lasted a bit longer, I believe I would have raised my grade to a B, as I did in my English class. As a result of these tutoring sessions and our lengthy talks afterward, we developed an unbreakable bond: Hillary became the sister I had wanted all my life.

While I was struggling with my computer class, Hillary was struggling with her Spanish class. I was eager to help her, so we'd work an hour on my computer and English lessons and then another hour on her Spanish lesson. She told me I didn't have to pay for her tutoring, since I was helping her with Spanish. No deal, because I knew she needed the money. We made a pact that she'd pay me once she landed a big position at a major corporation. The girl now speaks, reads, and writes Spanish better than most of my relatives.

The irrelevant and demeaning questions Hillary has been asked during job interviews on a path to nowhere are beyond my comprehension. The most important question should have been whether she could perform the job. For heaven's sake, she graduated with a 3.5 grade point average, compared with my measly 2.8. Yet it was I who got the best job opportunities after college. I'm viewed as the beautiful and exotic Latina with the thick accent; Hillary is viewed as the slightly overweight, smart Black woman with the nappy hair. My physical characteristics work in my favor, while Hillary's work to her detriment. But has Hillary ever shown any ill will toward me because of these racist and sexist realities? Not at all! She has celebrated my successes and, next to my mom, is my biggest cheerleader and supporter.

My relatives love Hillary and treat her as if she were born into our family. She loves them, too, especially my mom, who always tells her, "Hillary, you need a Latino man to spice up your life." She can't understand why some good Black man doesn't want a sweet, beautiful woman like Hillary. I can't understand it, either. We were clubbing together recently, and it angered the hell out of me when none of the brothers there asked Hillary to dance. She was dressed to the nines, and the girl has a knockout body, yet not one Black guy gave her a second look. They were falling all over themselves asking me or white girls to dance—never mind that some of the other girls were much heavier than and not nearly as attractive as Hillary.

I spoke to one brother who kept hitting on me:

"Hey, my fine Black brother, I think you might get to first base with me if you ask my friend to dance." That sawed-off sucker laughed and said, "My fine salsa sister, I am not desperate. There are too many other beautiful women I can ask to dance." I would have asked one of my wayward cousins to make him a eunuch, but we don't need any more Latino brothers in prison. Fortunately, one of my white brothers asked Hillary to dance without my prodding. They actually hit it off and danced the night away.

Funny thing about Hillary: even when she has an opportunity, she won't let any guy get too close. Don't even think about anyone going home with her for a night of passion. I haven't yet figured out her hesitation—every time I've tried to bring it up in the past, she's shut down—but I know one day she'll share with me whatever it is, in her own time.

10 DARRYL

My Plans Are Falling into Place

My workout at the gym today was one of the best ever. After seven hundred sit-ups and three hundred push-ups, I'm ready for a hot shower. My body is screaming for relief tonight. I constantly work to maintain a physique that makes the ladies take notice and drool a little, and I know the guys in the office are envious of my triceps and biceps—I can feel the stares when I take off my suit jacket in meetings, although they try to be discreet. I want to yell, *Eat your hearts out, you pathetic weaklings!*

My shower feels so good, and now it's sauna time. I'm taking my cell with me, since it's a secure place to engage in confidential discourse at this time of night, when no one's around. I have an important call coming from a very good friend. It's a call I wouldn't dare receive at home or at the office.

It's good to have friends you can count on when you need their support. The friend whose call I'm expecting, Joe Jayson, is a special investigator with the uncanny ability to access information on anybody in a timely fashion. His fees for maintaining the utmost confidentiality are downright extortionate, but he keeps his customers very happy.

I hope the burly beast who got his freak on while humiliating me that rainy night didn't think everything was over when he drove off in his patrol car. I replay the dreadful incident over and over in my head and get angrier each time I think about it. I gave Joe the cop's badge number and car number, and Joe assured me I'd have the guy's personal information sometime tonight. I'm getting impatient, but then my cell chimes with a text and Joe's secret code. This is his way of telling me it's okay to call him. I contact Joe on disposable cells we use for information sharing.

Man, it seems hotter than usual in the sauna. It doesn't matter, though. This call is important enough for me to roast for a while. Joe answers with his usual upbeat tone: "Hey, my rich Black brother, what's happening in the world of corporate greed? I have good news for my best customer. Your friend the police brute has a lot going on. I think you're going to sleep well tonight after I share what I've found out about him."

My heart races with anticipation; I won't rest until the burly cop feels the full impact of my wrath. Joe shares more information than I'll ever need for my payback scheme, including the burly cop's name, Nicolas Turner, although that doesn't matter—he'll always be the burly cop to me.

"Joe, you're the man. I owe you big-time," I say.

Joe answers, "Don't worry, my rich brother—you will pay me big-time. Just remember, you can always count on me to have your back."

Now I know everything about my burly antagonist. On the surface he appears to be a nice guy, instead of the sadistic brute who relished in deprecating and stripping me of my dignity. He has a wife and two sons and is a respected Boy Scout leader. And wouldn't you know it—he's also an elder in his church. But—uh-oh—he's also having an extramarital affair. I should have known he'd be one of those intransigent Christians who pray on Sunday and maliciously prey on the most vulnerable Monday through Saturday. It looks like he has a big event coming soon, the annual Boy Scouts Jubilee. He's one of the event leaders and is scheduled as the keynote speaker for the awards banquet.

It looks like he'll share why he chose the police force as a way to serve his community. His claim to fame is his commitment to being a positive role model for young Boy Scouts. He's also committed to purging the community of the bad guys who are a menace to society. Well said, you worthless savage—you may have won over many people with your patriotic, compassionate words, but you're about to experience humiliation in a manner that pales in comparison with what you put me through.

The special cell phone I used to glean all this information is courtesy of my psychotic and genius friend Frank Cook. He was one of the few people I befriended in college, and we've remained close. Frank graduated summa cum laude with a dual degree in physics and chemistry. The phone he created for me eradicates call traceability by dissolving like Jell-O when it's immersed in hot water and is then poured down the drain and washed into the abyss, never to be seen or used again.

Come to think of it, I need to call Frank before I dispose of the cell. Not only is the guy a whiz with innovative technical devices, he's also capable of mixing up the most interesting concoctions—some of which have been known to cause strange behaviors that shock the conscience. In other words, embarrassment doesn't begin to describe the devastation and personal ruin that Frank's chemicals can cause. Next to Joe, he's my most valuable and trusted ally.

Ultimately, I decide to wait and call Frank later in the week. The Scout Jubilee is a few weeks away, so I don't have to rush my plans. My body is also beginning to shrivel from the heat. Joe was right: I *will* rest better tonight than I have in several weeks. I love it when a plan comes together.

11 HILLARY

I Can't Believe My Ears

After only two months on the job, my team is assigned a project that could land a major contract for Sanger. I've been given a meaty assignment because of the confidence my team leader, Rick, has in my skills. While I'm working on a particular segment of the project, he decides I need access to secured documents stored in one of the remote supply areas. After I find the location, I discover there are multiple rooms in the area, and once I enter the access code, I head toward the back room, as Rick instructed.

While I'm in there, I hear multiple footsteps in the main area; then they stop near the corner where I'm working. It's obvious that whoever is there believes they're the only ones in the room. As they begin speaking, I recognize one of the two men as the awful John Griffin. He says to his companion, "We've got to get the arrogant Black bastard. His head has gotten too big. Do you see how he's walking around like a proud peacock since you hired the dumb blonde to work for him? He thinks he's so smart and doesn't realize he's going down. Mr. Darryl Kelsey, one day soon you will wish you had hired the Black chick, Hillary, instead of Cathy."

The other guy, none other than Jim Waters from HR, laughs and says, "Would you believe Darryl thinks we're friends? I record all of our conversations and have enough on the Black buzzard to get him fired today if I wanted, but that's too easy. It couldn't have worked better when he called me to take charge of recruiting his assistant, instead of the limp-wrist, Glenn. All Darryl needed was a watermelon to go with his wide grin when Cathy left his office." They laugh as Jim talks about dropping the bomb on Darryl once they get Cathy to file a sexual harassment claim against him.

John says, "How are you going to make that happen? She doesn't seem like the piece of trash you were hoping to hire. I think the dumb broad worships Mr. Kelsey. I tried to see if she would take my bait to gain some information about Darryl. She looked up at me with those adorable blue eyes and all but told me to go to hell."

Jim responds, "Maybe we can set her up so she has to go along with our plans. I can always threaten her with some bogus HR policy infraction. She's definitely not the brightest bulb on the Christmas tree."

John laughs but cautions, "Don't rush it. Let's

wait another three to four months so we can build a fail-proof case against him. I have to admit you outdid yourself in finding Cathy. She is a honey dripper. I'd like to get between those fine legs of hers."

Then Jim throws a bombshell at John: "You have enough on your hands with Sheryl."

John says with lots of pride. "Ever since Sheryl got that promotion, she's been keeping me very happy. I don't know how she's taking care of her old man *and* me. Not my worry. What I'd love to do is get ahold of that sweet little taco Lucia. Man, she lights my fire, but the snooty little immigrant won't give me the time of day. She hates Sheryl with a passion. Poor Sheryl—she tried to stand up for Lucia, but I told her no little immigrant is going to get promoted under my watch. All I have to do to keep Sheryl under control is mention a possible cutback in staffing. She needs her job, so she kisses up to me and does whatever I tell her to do. It's great and is almost like having a personal sex slave. You should try it, Jim. Bet you got your eye on Glenn, though."

It's clear to me that Jim doesn't like John's comment. "Hey, man, don't put the gay mantle on me. I'm as straight as the road to hell."

They both laugh. I'm in a total freeze frame and praying they don't walk any farther and discover me in the remote corner. I can only imagine what they would conjure up about me. I don't want to get fired from my new job I love so much. I realize I've barely been breathing almost the entire time they've been talking. They need to leave soon, before I pass out. After talking about John's weekend with Sheryl, they finally bring their wicked conversation to an end, but only after deciding they'll meet at the same time next week to further lay out their plans to bring down Darryl.

I'm in a state of complete shock after they leave the room. I'm afraid to move, in case Jim or John is still lurking nearby. Is this what being a leader in corporate America is all about—people stabbing each other in the back and holding women hostage for sexual favors? Those two rogues are probably used to meeting in this room with no one around. They're too absorbed in their planning to bother checking the area to ensure they're alone.

After about half an hour, I finish my work and return to my cubicle. I'm shaking like a leaf on a windy March day in Chicago when I get to my desk. Many people don't believe in demons. They would change their minds after meeting those two.

I've got to talk to Lucia about this. She'll know what to do. My head is still reeling from the thought that these guys are hell-bent on destroying Darryl, and primarily because he's Black.

What's wrong with me? Why should I care what happens to Darryl—Mr. Kelsey? He treated me like a piece of moldy bread, and here I am, feeling the need to protect him from those two vultures—the same man who totally dissed me and hired a lesser-skilled blonde. It's just like Black women to try and rescue Black men who treat us like garbage. Lord knows I have enough troubles of my own without taking on someone else's. Mr. Kelsey adores his lovely Cathy, so let her look out for him. I'm going to purge my mind of this drama. Yes, that's what I'm going to do. To hell with Mr. Darryl Kelsey! I couldn't care less that he's headed for a big fall.

12 DARRYL

The Payback Plans Continue

My high school reunion is less than a month away. I had Cathy make my hotel and car reservations. I can't wait to see how life has treated my old classmates, especially Charles and Sally. I hear he's done well for himself: great job, beautiful wife, and he's highly regarded in his community. I also hear he's gained weight but is still quite the handsome charmer. Yes, I'm sure he thinks he's still king of the hill, but the person he least expects has dethroned him. I saw a recent photo of Sally, and she's Ms. High Society. She looks as beautiful as ever, is happily married to a wealthy doctor, and has four children. We'll see how happy she is after the reunion. Both she and Charles are on the list of attendees. Life really is going to get better for me.

My disposable cell phone rings, and the caller ID shows my friend Frank Cook's name. Frank gives me his usual loud and boisterous greeting: "My good friend, how are you? What miracle do I need to perform this time?"

We both laugh and I say, "My good man, I hope life is treating you as well as always. I need to know if the unique and potent product we've used in the past is still obtainable."

Frank say, "You're in luck. It's not only still available but more powerful than ever." I explain where and when I need it, and good ol' Frank says, "You can count on me to come through with a new and improved product. I've never failed you in the past and don't intend to do so in the future. My magic will exceed your expectations once again." We exchange good-byes and end the call.

Okay, now I have to make sure I'm registered for the upcoming high school reunion. I decide to call the reunion coordinator, a phony woman I couldn't stand when we were in school together and still can't tolerate now. "Edith," I say, "I'm confirming my reunion reservations and want to make sure you included my bio in the dinner program."

She's syrupy sweet when she assures me my very impressive bio is included. "Darryl, we are so excited about your support and thank you so very much for your generous donation to the reunion foundation. You are a true gem." The syrup continues to pour, and I'm close to gagging. "You will, of course, have prominent seating, and I will personally be at your beck and call."

My beck and call? Who's she kidding? She's hoping to get over with me, but she's definitely not my type.

She shows her hand when she says, "You haven't responded yet about your guest. I want to make sure she feels welcome and right at home." Now she's being nosy, trying to slyly learn who's going to be my reunion date. I can hear her now, calling her friends as soon as we hang up. Too bad, Ms. Nosy Edith, you're in for a surprise like everyone else. No, I'm not telling you anything about my date. It'll be one of the reunion shockers.

"I appreciate your concern for my guest," I tell her, "but that's a decision yet to come. Thanks for your assistance with my registration." I immediately hang up without giving her a chance to respond.

If this woman only knew what I think of her and what's being planned for her dear reunion, she'd probably run like hell from me. What an interesting time will be had by all. Those who scorned me in the past won't believe their eyes when they see Mr. Darryl Kelsey. I can't wait to give my special treat to Charles. I've tried to stop hating him, but it just won't happen. He caused me so much pain that for-giveness is not in the picture. I'm still on the fence about what to do with Sally, but I know it will be as enjoyable as my gift to Charles.

It's time I selected my guest for this special event. I call one of the women, Carol White, who enjoys attending special functions with me. She's the perfect eye candy for the reunion. I can hear the sisters whispering now. They will experience lots of regret for having treated me like a rabid dog while we were in school. No, actually, I know dogs that get better treatment—I was treated like the rotten garbage my father loaded onto his truck.

Carol answers and chides me for not having called her for a couple of months. I really don't care much for her, but she serves the right purpose whenever I need her. "Hi, Carol. I'm sorry we haven't talked in a while. You know I've been busy with major projects at work. But I'm planning to attend my high school reunion next month and checking to see if you'd like to be my guest. It's a weekend event and should be most enjoyable."

Carol eagerly responds, "I'd love to go. I assume we'll be sharing a hotel room. It's just a few weeks away, and I have to decide what to wear. Is there a theme?"

I'm not sure why Carol mentioned her attire— that's *my* decision. "You've never had to decide what to wear when I've invited you to an event. I've always selected and paid for your outfits, and this time won't be any different. Are you still the same size four?" Carol knows if she's gone up a size, I won't allow her to attend the reunion with me. That's the reason I keep several white women as ready companions. Carol assures me she's still the same size, so I say, "I'll have the dresses and accessories delivered to you. You know the drill: wear only the outfits I've purchased for this event. The bright side for you is you get to keep these items. Does that still work for you?"

Carol sighs. "Of course, Darryl. I know the drill, and it works for me."

I share the travel itinerary, and Carol asks, "Darryl, do you think we can get together prior to the trip? I'd love to spend some quality time with you to catch up." Why she asks this, I don't know. Carol knows she serves one purpose for me, and that's being on call for a date when I need her, but I string her along a bit and throw out a date she and I both know I'll cancel. She gives me a kiss through the phone and says good-bye.

This will probably be the last time Carol has the pleasure of my company. She's lucky I've tolerated her for over a year. That's a long time for me to keep a woman as part of my small collection of disposable companions. I usually take them out to dinner for a test-drive, and then, if they meet my expectations for dress, etiquette, speech, figure, and appropriate admiration, they'll stick around for about six months.

These women always want to move to a sexual relationship, but that's not part of the game. People would be shocked to learn I'm still a virgin, by choice. I like to have a beautiful white woman on my arm for special effect, but not in my bed. I love the way it pisses off the sisters and the white guys.

That's the main reason I date white women; otherwise, I have no interest in them at all.

I haven't found the right woman for my bed. I am not a homosexual; I'm a man with tremendous discipline. Many a man has stumbled because of his inability to control sexual urges. That will not be the case for me, Darryl Kelsey. My parents should have named me Disciplined Darryl Kelsey. I can only imagine the ridicule I would have suffered from my high school classmates for that name.

I do have to thank my classmates for one thing: they taught me the patience and perseverance to deal with a lot of hard knocks in my life. I've pulled myself together through many a tough trial. I'm in control now, and I do mean *control*.

13 LUCIA

How Do We Outsmart the Schemers?

I'm sitting in the Great Earth restaurant, waiting for Hillary. She called me this afternoon and sounded pretty desperate. Actually, "frantic" is a more appropriate description. She insisted we meet urgently, and I'm beyond curious about what's going on. I hope she hasn't done anything to jeopardize her job. So far, Michael and his staff have loved having her on the team.

I'm grateful Michael hired Hillary. He's a good man, and I'm overjoyed he's my friend. We would do anything for each other, and I owe him big-time for hiring Hillary. I would absolutely die if things went south after I gave him rave reviews about her skills and abilities. He says we're now even because I've always had his back. Hey, that's what friends are for.

Hillary would curse the ground I walk on if she knew I intervened to get her this job. The white guys do it all the time, so why shouldn't I? At least

Hillary is highly competent. Those guys routinely hire friends, family members, and friends of family members into the company. Many of them often lack basic competencies, but no one says a thing. They get on-the-job training from minority and retirement-eligible employees who are paid less than the people they're training. Those same employees are then passed over for promotions they deserve.

Let a person of color bring in a friend or family member, and those same guys are quick to run to Ethics to complain about preferential treatment. You want to see preferential treatment, go look at the company organization chart and you'll see that 98 percent of the leaders are white males, with a white woman or two and usually a Black male thrown in to show that Sanger is committed to diversity. Its real definition of diversity is white men with different-colored hair and degrees from different universities.

I'm getting depressed thinking about it, so I'm glad when Hillary shows up. She's out of breath and barely seated before she blurts out, "You won't believe what I heard today in one of the supply areas. I thought I knew wicked, but there's a new definition of the term lurking at Sanger."

"Okay, my sister—calm down, take a deep breath, and tell me what happened." We carry on our conversation in Spanish. When I arrived at the restaurant, I made sure we were in a private area where we could talk without being overheard, even if we're speaking Spanish. I trust very few people, and you can never be too careful these days, since Spanish is no longer spoken solely by Hispanics. Hillary is the perfect example of how things have changed.

Hillary recounts what she heard from the two clowns, and I'm not shocked. "Lucia, the vile and revolting John called Sheryl his sex slave. I almost vomited at the thought. I think she's tried to look out for you, but the creep won't let her. Can you imagine the evil those two have conjured up? Oh, one more thing, but don't you gag on me: John wants to get close to you. He calls you his 'sweet little taco.'"

I'm fuming and feeling both indignation and the urge to kill, so I begin to rant. "I know they're capable of all kinds of evil. I've watched them try to destroy Michael. John had the audacity to spread rumors about Michael having a sexual preference for young boys. That was totally false. Michael should have sued them for slander, but he's too nice. Just as they were careless in their conversation this time, the same thing happened with their last episode. I became aware of their wicked scheme and, after giving Michael a heads-up, helped him devise his own plan to work against them. Those two dirt bags 'almost' lost their jobs.

"It never ceases to amaze me that if I had sunk to

their level and committed one-quarter of their deviousness, I would have been fired in a hot minute. Those guys are like the phoenix—they always rise from the ashes. I don't get it. Top management has always forgiven their sins, so they feel untouchable. They've experienced privilege all their lives and don't have a clue about personal integrity."

Hillary quietly comments, "You know I can't stand Darryl Kelsey. The man hates me for no reason. Yet it's hard for me to sit back and allow those two jerks to destroy him."

Unlike Hillary, I have to admit the thought of someone taking down Mr. Darryl Kelsey did resonate with me at first, but that's not right. I'm ashamed of those bad thoughts. Hillary's such a good Christian girl and wants to do the right thing by everyone. I know she won't rest until we do something to help Darryl, so I say, "Well, my sister, figuring out what to do to protect Darryl is the million-dollar question. We don't have a complete picture of what the two jackasses are up to, but we know they're trying to make Cathy part of their evil plan. The other big question is whether Cathy will allow herself to be used by those jerks. You seem confident Cathy doesn't have a clue about their devious scheme."

My thoughts drift back to John and Sheryl, and those thoughts become audible. "I'm in shock that John is referring to Sheryl as his sex slave. I almost feel sorry for her. You'd think she would have more pride than to lie with a snake like John. Yuck! The thought of that slimeball having sex with me makes me want to upchuck. He has a hell of a lot of nerve, bringing me into his sexual fantasies. If anyone needs to be taken down, it's John Griffin. He's the true devil on Earth."

Hillary nods in agreement and says, "This time around, we have to make sure John and Jim get what's coming to them. Evil deserves to be put down, and I do mean *down*!"

I'm surprised at these words coming from Hillary. She always gives everyone second, third, and fourth chances. "You go, girl—for once, we're in agreement on bringing evil down." We do the Obamas' fist-bump to punctuate our solidarity.

We decide to learn more about Cathy. Hillary already has an opening to build a relationship with her, since Cathy has complained several times to her that she's felt as if some assignments were over her head. Hillary seems more surprised than anything else that Cathy, who started off worshiping Darryl, has been opening up to her so much, but to me this is the perfect opportunity for these two women to form an alliance that could benefit all of us. With those thoughts in mind, I share a plan with Hillary. "Listen, girl, you need to offer to help Cathy and befriend her during the process to build a trusting relationship. You should share some fictitious, secret stories about your life as a way to get Cathy to talk about her private life. Let's take advantage of your loving personality. This has to start tomorrow."

I'm now on a roll: "We'll monitor the movements of the two demons to track their meeting times. If there's a pattern to those times, then we can strategize about an approach to eavesdrop on future conversations and learn more about their devilish scheme. I'd love to make sure those two are walked out the door for good this time. As far as saving Darryl goes, I'll have to think long and hard about that."

Hillary tries not to smile but can't help herself. I love her good heart. For her sake, I'll give serious thought to helping Darryl, even though I wouldn't mind if we took down all three of those clowns.

We finish our meals and complete our conversation still speaking Spanish, which is how Hillary stays sharp at the language. Thank God for my dear friend. What would I do without her in my life? I hope I never find out.

14 DARRYL

Keeping Everything on Track

It's early morning, and I call my friend Frank Cook to once again go over every detail of tomorrow's plan. Mr. Burly Cop is still scheduled to deliver the keynote message at the evening banquet. The program shows him speaking around seven o'clock. This is the biggest Scout event of the year, with over two hundred Scouts and their families and friends in attendance from all over the state. Counting the local and state dignitaries, roughly 750 people will be present.

Once I'm satisfied with the details, a strong sense of anticipation overtakes my anxiety. I'm glad that Sanger agreed to cover the cost of videotaping this event as part of our sponsorship, which landed us a prime table. None of the vice presidents wanted to attend the banquet, so they gave the tickets to me to distribute among my team. Strong representation from Sanger at this event is a must. Community relations are very important for our company image, even if our leaders couldn't care less about Scouting or most other community initiatives.

After having tossed and turned all night thinking about the Scout dinner, I decide to go for a run to ease my nerves. It's a nice, crisp morning, and the sun is shining brightly. I hope it's a good sign for me, because rain has spelled trouble for me in the recent past. For some strange reason, I begin to think about the burly cop's family. How will they deal with the embarrassment he's going to face and that ultimately they will face? Why should I care? He certainly wasn't concerned about the embarrassment he caused me that rainy night. No, it's unfortunate, but there is always collateral damage during times of war, and I've declared war against Mr. Burly Cop. I decide to run a few extra miles to ease the tension before I head to work.

I arrive at the office a little later than usual, but Cathy greets me with her usual sweet smile, "Hello, Mr. Kelsey. I've already gotten your latte, and it's nice and hot, waiting for you on your desk. May I get anything else for you this morning?"

I thank Cathy and tell her I'm fine. I am overjoyed with her. I couldn't ask for a better assistant. She seems a little frustrated at times, but she's just a bit rusty; I'm sure her skills will improve. I have to make sure I do something special for Jim Waters for doing an A-plus job in recruiting Cathy. He's really got my back, and I'm glad I don't have to work with that punk Glenn Hendricks. I don't trust him as far as I can throw him.

Later in the day, as I walk out of my office, I'm surprised to see Hillary Montgomery chatting with Cathy. What the hell is Hillary doing in this area? She doesn't belong on this floor. I don't want Cathy to have anything to do with that woman. She never should have been hired. I don't care about all the good things Michael and his team say about her. It's early yet, and she'll soon show her true colors.

I literally step between the two of them and turn my back on Hillary, ignoring her as I interrupt their conversation. "Cathy, I need you to run these documents over to John Griffin's office and he needs them right now." I emphasize "now."

Cathy immediately ends her conversation with Hillary. She sends an apologetic look Hillary's way, takes the papers, and heads for the elevator. Hillary shoots a displeased look at me when our eyes meet momentarily. I turn abruptly to go back into my office as she walks away.

I hope Hillary got the message I don't want her in or near my office area. Who knows what her conniving kind is up to? Black women have always been nothing but trouble for me. I will have to watch out for this misfit and make sure she stays in her place—which is nowhere near my office or my assistant.

I knew from the minute Hillary first walked into my office for her job interview that she was trouble. She's clever, and there's something evil lurking underneath that sweet smile and kind words she has for everyone. Cathy is very innocent and vulnerable to a conniving witch like Hillary, who camouflages her wickedness. I have to protect Cathy from Hillary so that she doesn't become an instrument for Hillary to carry out her evil schemes against me. Michael had the nerve to tell me that he hired a star when he hired Hillary. Total BS! It's too soon for him to come to that conclusion anyway— she's been on the job less than two months—but what can you expect from a bleeding-heart liberal like Michael?

I call Cathy into my office when she returns from delivering the documents to John. She looks as if she's close to tears, so I'd better put her at ease. "I'm sorry, Cathy, that I abruptly ended your conversation with Hillary. I wasn't trying to be rude, but there's a lot going on right now and I don't want anyone getting the wrong impression that you have the time to engage in conversations unrelated to the tasks at hand. I appreciate your understanding and hope you know you're a breath of fresh air around here. It's a pleasure to have someone who goes the extra mile to make sure everything is in place for her boss. I can't thank you enough for all you do for me and for Sanger. You are one of the best hires I've made in my career."

Cathy now smiles, nods her head, and says, "I understand."

I smile at her and give her a warm nod of dismissal, and she walks back to her desk.

I think I handled that well. Cathy is the perfect assistant, and I don't want to do anything that might cause her to have second thoughts about working for me. She may not have great skills, but she knows how to treat Mr. Darryl Kelsey, and that's all that matters. Of course, it helps that she's great eye candy for my colleagues and clients.

Just then, Cathy buzzes me on the intercom and tells me she has to make a trip to the ladies' room. What if men had to make as many trips to the men's room as women make to the ladies' room? Maybe she's on her menstrual cycle, which would account for her being close to tears. Women are so fragile when they're on their period. I'll make a note of this date on my calendar and will remember to be gentler with Cathy in the future around this time of the month. Shame on me for not having noticed this earlier.

15 HILLARY

Mr. Darryl Kelsey, Who Do You Think You Are?

I leave Mr. Kelsey's area in a huff after yet another display of disrespectful treatment. The man is a raving idiot and a world-class jerk. It's hard to believe he just gave me the invisible-Black-woman treatment. He had the nerve to interrupt the conversation between Cathy and me. The jerk actually turned his back to me as he spoke to her! He truly has issues. He acted as if Cathy were the only person standing there beside him. I'm so angry I could march back to his office and scream a few obscenities at him, but I can't afford to lose my job.

I head straight to the restroom to have a little talk with Jesus, because I'm at the end of my rope with this man. Great—the restroom is empty, so it's just Jesus and me. "Lord, you know I am your committed and humble servant. Please reveal to me whatever I've done to displease you and led to my having to deal with the likes of Darryl Kelsey. I ask for your immediate forgiveness so he can be removed from my life. Lord, I came so close today to putting my foot up his starched Black...uh, behind. I'm so glad you have given me the gift of calmness. I don't know why Darryl has what appears to be a deep-seated hatred for Black women. Only you and Darryl know why, but I'm guessing his mother must have abused or abandoned him as a child. Maybe some sister he insulted didn't have you in her life and scalded him with hot grits. Maybe I should let John Griffin and Jim Waters eat him alive...but I know that's not what you would have me do. You placed me in an environment where he lurks for a reason I can't yet conceive. I trust you and know you'll see me through this trial, as you have all others. I may need an extra dose of self-control every now and then, because this situation is testing my Christian core. You're a good God, and I love you with all my heart, my mind, my strength, and my soul. Amen."

I feel better now, and as I'm leaving, Cathy comes into the restroom. She has a sad look on her face as she turns to me and says, "Hillary, I'm so sorry for what happened this morning. Mr. Kelsey has a major project with extremely tight deadlines, and I think the pressure got to him this morning. I'm sure he didn't mean to ignore or disrespect you."

I'm taken aback by Cathy's defense of Darryl's behavior. There are no excuses for his actions toward me this morning. He in fact was also being disrespectful to Cathy by totally disregarding her conversation with me. I can't stand by and let her defend him, so I say, "Cathy, I appreciate your loyalty to Mr. Darryl Kelsey, but please don't make excuses for his rudeness. The man doesn't like me, and he's determined to make sure I know it. It took everything within me to keep from popping him in the mouth, but I want to keep my job and it also wouldn't have been the Christian thing to do."

Cathy starts to speak but decides not to, and then the tears start flowing. I feel badly and put my arm around her shoulder as I say, "Cathy, please don't take my comments as directed toward you. You don't know how much it means for you to come in here and apologize to me when you've done nothing wrong. I just had to let off some steam, and I'm sorry if I hurt your feelings. I really am."

Cathy shakes her head and says, "Hillary, my tears are flowing because I should have said something. I stood there and acted like a robot, which is how I've always acted with my bosses. Don't get me wrong, Mr. Kelsey treats me well, but, as I've shared with you before, his demands can be very frustrating for me because of some of my skill limitations. He has such high standards, and I'm doing everything possible to try and keep up. You don't know how much I appreciate the help you've given me when I've been in a deadline crunch. Mr. Kelsey would fire me on the spot if he knew this, but please know how much I appreciate you. He recently complimented me on work that you performed. I feel like I've let you down."

I smile at Cathy and say, "You have not let me down, and I didn't expect you to speak on my behalf. We both did the right thing at the time. I walked away, and you took the document to John Griffin. By the way, the work we do together is between you and me. No one else has to know, and I would never tell a soul."

Cathy gives me a hug and says, "I thank you for being so kind to me. I don't know what I would do without you. I don't want either of us to run afoul of Mr. Kelsey, so maybe it's best we meet after work. How about sometime next week? Let me know when you're available, because I'm pretty flexible."

I return Cathy's hug and let her know that I'll check my schedule for a time next week. My team has a heavy workload right now.

Then Cathy looks at her watch and panics. "I'd better get back to my desk. Mr. Kelsey doesn't like me gone too long, and I don't want to upset him." I shake my head. The jerk is a controlling chauvinist pig, but I keep this thought to myself. No need to stress Cathy out any more than she is right now with something I'm sure she already knows.

As we walk out of the restroom, I feel an inexplicable bond with Cathy and a good feeling about this new connection. I know Lucia's not too keen on her, but I'm a good judge of character. I see Cathy as a good human being, and I don't believe those two demons will be able to use her against Darryl, even though she seems to really care for Darryl in a professional way. I will help Cathy, not as part of a scheme to gain information, but to return the kindness and respect she's shown me. I feel better already. *Thank you, God, for the way you bring peace and calmness when I'm all worked up over the devil's children at Sanger who are hell-bent on stealing my joy.*

16 LUCIA

The Project of a Lifetime

When I arrive at work the morning after Hillary and I concoct our plan about Cindy, I'm surprised to find Sheryl waiting outside my office, wearing the sweetest, phoniest smile. She's syrupy sweet, and greets me with a level of warmth and caring that she's never shown in any of our past interactions.

"Good morning, Lucia. I hope all is well in your life. John Griffin and I would like to meet with you at nine o'clock this morning in his office. I hope you don't have a schedule conflict. If you do, I'm sure you can move things around. See you at nine."

The two of them are obviously up to something. Sheryl has given me the cold shoulder ever since I filed that complaint against her. She usually converses with me only when she has to give instructions or needs something. As she sashays away, I can feel the bile rising in my throat. I want to scream out, *You're nothing but a lowly sex slave, so don't talk down to me*! but I control my emotions and instead begin dialing Hillary's cell.

"Hey, girl, say one of those special prayers for me this morning. I have a meeting at nine o'clock with John and Sheryl."

"Oh my God!" Hillary shrieks. "In the name of Jesus, please protect my sister from the two evil ones."

We both laugh, and she asks me to call her as soon as I get out of the meeting, but I don't trust this environment to discuss the details, so I tell her, "Not a good idea. Let's meet this evening. Stop by my place after work, and we'll talk then. I'll call you when I'm leaving the office. Love you, my sister!"

Hillary says, "Love you, too. Are you wearing a cross? I think I'll call my mother and ask her to have her prayer warriors start praying."

I laugh again. "No, and I don't think they're going to do much harm."

I hang up and head to John's office. His assistant tells me that he and Sheryl are waiting for me. As I walk in, John is friendlier than I've ever seen him in the past seven years. "Hi, Lucia. Thanks for meeting with us." As if I had a choice. "We have some good news to share with you. I'm sure you remember the Spanish company Castillo Information Systems. We almost landed a contract with them over a year ago, and you played a key role in preparing it. Unfortunately, we lost the business to one of our competitors. Well, they're not happy and are terminating that contract. The good news is, they'd like to give us another chance. Isn't that great?"

I nod my head, but I'm in disbelief that these two idiots have the nerve to think I'd be excited, given the way they treated me after we lost the contract last year. Still, I need my job, so I try to play along with them.

John continues, "Lucia, since you played a key role in the last effort, we want you to lead the project this time around. This means an immediate promotion for you to lead project manager, along with a significant salary increase. You'll be able to assemble the talent you need to make this important opportunity a success. You'll also have our full support. How does this sound to you?"

"Sounds like a great opportunity for Sanger and for me," I mumble. Then I pull myself together and sound more enthusiastic. "I'm pleased with your confidence in my ability to lead this project. I'm eager to get all of the details so I can pull the right team together."

John smiles and says, "That's what we were hoping to hear. The Castillo team will be here next week, and I'll get the statement of work to you by close of business tomorrow."

I'm still in a state of skepticism, combined with some hesitation, since I don't trust those two, but I thank John and go back to my office in a fog. Sheryl didn't say a word the entire meeting, so I ignored her as best I could without appearing disrespectful. John always keeps her mute, but for the life of me I don't know why she puts up with that chauvinist pig. Oh well—that's the problem with being a sex slave.

I can't wait to share the news with Hillary. That girl's prayers are truly powerful. This opportunity has been a long time coming, and I walk purposefully around my office to make sure I'm not dreaming. I really don't want to be disappointed again, and I wish there was a way to confirm what I just heard.

Glenn's call breaks through my thoughts and provides what I need. "Hi, Lucia, and congratulations! I'm sure you've heard the good news by now. By the way, the promotion comes with a twenty-five percent salary increase, and you're also being moved to a larger office. I couldn't be happier for you."

With that, I transition from shock to euphoria. "Thanks, Glenn. I can't tell you how much I appreciate the help you've given me over the years. You truly are the heart and soul of Sanger."

I can practically feel Glenn blushing. "Ah, Lucia, I just try to do what's right. It helps that you're one of my favorite people." We agree to meet later in the week to discuss my change of status.

I get through the rest of the day still in a fog

and look forward to sharing the good news with my family and Hillary. As I drive home, I think of how proud my mother will be when I tell her about my promotion. She's always been in my corner, and since Dad passed, our bond has grown even deeper. She's a believer in celebrations, so I expect a huge Hernandez family gathering. There's nothing that compares to these get-togethers; everyone talks at once, but the strange thing is, we all understand one another. The food will be off the chain—lots of authentic Mexican dishes, including the tamales that my mom and her sisters prepare by the dozen at Christmastime and freeze so we can enjoy them throughout the year. My uncle Jaime makes the best margaritas and sangria punch. They'll toast to "our" success, because any personal accomplishment for a Hernandez is an accomplishment for the whole family.

When I pull up in front of the house, I see that Hillary's car is already parked there, and I know she and my mom are talking up a storm. I remember the first time she joined one of the Hernandez family dinners. My cousin Raul, not knowing that Hillary speaks Spanish, said loudly to some of the men, "*Amo a hermanas Negras finas con un poco de carne en sus huesos.*" ("I love fine Black sisters with a little meat on their bones.")

You could have scraped him off the floor when Hillary responded in perfect Spanish, "Thank you so much. I also love fine Hispanic brothers with a little meat on their bones." It was the first time we'd ever seen him at a total loss for words. He still hasn't fully recovered from the teasing the family bombarded him with, especially my other macho cousins, but Hillary was such a good sport about it that now they're the best of buddies. Mom has even tried not-so-subtle matchmaking with them. I just wish Hillary wouldn't be so uptight when it comes to romance. I'll never stop hoping that one day she'll open up about whatever keeps her from allowing Mr. Right to come into her life.

As I open the door, all the love just pours out to greet me. Hillary speaks first: "*Hola, mi hermana. ¿Que has tardado tanto?*"

I laugh and say, "What do you mean, what took me so long? I drove like a maniac through all this traffic so I could share my latest news."

Of course my mother joins the conversation right away: "What news? Don't tell me you're pregnant with my grandchild!"

"No, Mother, I'm not pregnant and don't plan to be for some time, thank you very much. I'd like to have a husband first! Please let me set my things down and get a drink of water. I promise to tell you my news right after that."

As I'm getting settled, I can see and feel the anticipation from my mother and Hillary. Even once we sit around the kitchen table, I feel like teasing them a bit more, so I say, "Well, today my supervisor, who hasn't communicated with me other than to give me assignments, asked me to meet in her boss's office this morning. I was scared to death because this woman smiled when she spoke to me, and I felt chills all over my body."

Mother is so anxious. "Get to the point, sweetheart—we don't need all the background details."

"Okay. I was promoted to lead a major project with the Spanish company we lost a contract with last year. The company doesn't like the current contractor and decided to give Sanger another chance. I'm getting a big raise, and I get to select the people on my team."

"I'm so happy for you!" Hillary says, as she gives me a big hug. "You are so deserving, and everyone admires you at Sanger. I often hear comments about you being the most underrated talent at Sanger."

My mother is ecstatic and has tears in her eyes as she showers me with hugs and kisses. "I'm so proud of you, sweetheart. Oh, your dad is smiling down on you from heaven."

Hillary suggests we go out to dinner because this news is worthy of a big-time celebration. Mother isn't too happy about that suggestion, since, sure enough, she's already prepared a nice meal to eat at home, but she relents and we leave for my uncle's restaurant. On the way there, Mother talks on her cell to her sister Marcia, which means the entire Hernandez family will know about my good fortune before we even reach the restaurant. But I don't care—I'm so happy right now, and it feels good to have my mother and my best friend equally happy. I'm getting an opportunity I've long awaited to work on one of the most important projects in the Sanger portfolio. ¡*Aleluya!* As Hillary often says, "God is truly good!"

17 DARRYL

The Hour Draws Near

The rain is pouring, and I'm sinking farther and farther into the mud; it's now up to my neck. The burly white cop is laughing, joined by the other cops. I hear him saying, "He should begin suffocating anytime now."

I begin screaming, "Somebody help me! Somebody help me!" as the mud rises to my chin. The cars just whiz by, and nobody's paying any attention to me as the cops wave them on. The mud continues to rise, until it's right below my lower lip. I start screaming, "Where's the God that's supposed to be helping me? Please don't let me die." But even He doesn't hear me. Then I feel myself swallowing mud and can no longer scream.

A loud ringing sound wakes me from this horrible dream. I've never welcomed the sound of my alarm clock the way I do this morning. As I reach out and shut it off, I notice I'm wringing wet with sweat, as my body was fighting a sure death. I feel this intense sense of relief, and I'm so happy I was only dreaming, yet I experience a sense of dread as these recurring dreams bring me closer to death. It's as if the burly cop wasn't satisfied with the agony he caused me on that rainy night. He has somehow gained a stronghold in my subconscious and now regularly invades my dreams as I sleep.

Let's hope tonight's banquet will provide the ultimate cure for these nightmares. The thought brings a level of satisfaction that surpasses what I experienced when I hired Cathy as my assistant. Yes, tonight's the night!

I get dressed for work and decide to lay out a suit and accessories to change into for tonight's banquet. I wish I could fast-forward the time, but I have to make sure everything is in place for flawless execution—and I do mean Darryl Kelsey's method of execution. I've tried to avoid being a vindictive person, but this guy has to feel the pain I've felt during and since that rainy night.

It's appropriate that today is a cloudy day. As I pull into my parking space and then walk toward the building, I'm hoping it rains like hell tonight. The elevator is full, as usual, and as I step out on the twenty-second floor, I'm surprised to see Lucia Hernandez up here. She rarely comes to the C-suite. I wonder what brings her by. She is drop-dead gorgeous and flashes her beautiful smile as she speaks to me. "Hi, Mr. Kelsey. Thanks for inviting me to the Boy Scout banquet tonight. The Boy Scouts is such a worthy organization, and I'm glad Sanger is a supporter. It's really great to have someone at your level attend this event."

I smile and say, "It's my pleasure to attend, and I'm glad you're going. It should be a fun night. Michael Dunlap is coming, as well as Glenn Hendricks from HR. Glenn was a Boy Scout as a child." I don't say I hate like hell that I have to spend an evening with two homosexuals; I keep that to myself. Tonight, I don't care who goes, as long as my plan is executed to perfection.

As soon as I sit down at my desk, John Griffin walks into my office, sporting a devilish grin that says he's up to something. "Hey, Boss, I've got everything in motion to meet the deadline for the Castillo contract revision. I can't believe the bastards are giving us just four weeks to get our proposal together."

I nod and say, "Keep in mind this contract brings big bucks for Sanger, and Castillo has the bucks. It's a crazy timeline, but we have to meet it. What plans do you have in motion?"

John smirks as he says, "You're right, Boss. We're giving the project lead to the adorable Latina Lucia. She's always asking for meaningful work, and now she's going to get it."

I can't believe my ears. "Lucia! Have you forgotten what happened with her complaints after the last proposal? Are you insane?"

John attempts to reassure me. "Sheryl and I met with Lucia this morning. She's onboard with becoming the project lead. I told her about the promotion, and she was very appreciative. Of course, I didn't let Sheryl say one word."

"John, I don't get it. Lucia can't handle this project alone. Does she know about the tight deadline and who's assigned to work with her?"

"She doesn't have the details yet. We're meeting tomorrow morning, and I'll explain all the essentials to her then. She gets to select her team, and I've assured her of our full support. Of course, we want her to be successful."

This is not the real John Griffin talking right now. He would never want a woman or a person of color to succeed, so I'll have to watch this carefully. "I want a full report after you speak with Lucia," I say. "This project has to be successful. The buck stops with me. If this project fails, you and I have a real problem. Understood?"

John is all smiles. "Hey, Boss, I've got your back. It will be successful. I'll schedule an appointment with Cathy to update you once everything is in place with Lucia.

"By the way, Cathy is really something. I think you hit a home run when you hired her. Is she doing a good job?"

I wonder why he's asking. "She's doing an excellent job, but I'm not concerned with Cathy right now. My concern is that we get the proposal in the hands of Castillo within four weeks—on time or ahead of time!"

John smiles again and nods. "Don't worry, Boss, we'll make sure Lucia has everything she needs to make the project a success. And I'll see you at dinner tonight—my son was an Eagle Scout, so Molly and I are excited about the banquet. Thanks for the invitation."

I watch John leave my office, all the while thinking I'll have to learn much more about the project deliverables and make sure it's a success. I don't trust John at all. He puts on his best face for me, but something tells me that he's always up to no good. I just don't feel right about his decision to make Lucia the project lead. I know it's time to get better acquainted with her, but I can't think that far ahead right now, with the big night rapidly approaching.

18 DARRYL

One Down, One to Go

The rain is coming down much harder than the Weather Channel predicted. What a perfect night for payback. The ladies at the reception table for the Boy Scouts banquet whisper to each other when I walk up. They look a little surprised to see this handsome Black man approaching the table. The man in line ahead of me gets a cheerful greeting from one of them—"Hello, sir, and welcome to the annual Boy Scouts Jubilee. Your name is?"—while the other one seems to decide it's her chore to deal with me.

In the pithy tone that typifies many people's reactions to a Black male in a predominantly white setting, she says, "How may I help you?"

I just smile and give her my name. "I'm Mr. Darryl Kelsey, representing Sanger, the platinum sponsor for this event."

It's amazing how big-money sponsorship buys a Black man superficial respect. They immediately jump to attention. "Mr. Kelsey, we have you at the Sanger table. How nice to see you."

One of the ladies on the side, who's overheard my name in conjunction with Sanger's, runs over to greet me and almost embraces me. "Oh, hello, Mr. Kelsey. Welcome! We are delighted that you're here. We're so appreciative of Sanger's generosity. Please, let me take you to your table."

As I'm being ushered to the Sanger table, I quickly scan the ballroom and notice a 98 percent white audience. I stand out in more ways than one. First and foremost, I'm the best-dressed man in the ballroom. As we reach the table, just as I'm taking my seat, Ms. Banquet Hostess introduces me to some local dignitaries who are walking by. I see surprised looks when she mentions that I'm a Sanger executive vice president. They were obviously expecting someone representing the company who looks a lot different from me. Fortunately, the burly cop is busy elsewhere and misses my introduction. I don't want him to know I'm in the room—as if he'd remember me. I'm sure I was just another Black face for him to harass.

The room is packed, and even the mayor is here, which is a surprise, since he's not up for reelection for two more years. I didn't vote for the scoundrel, but he toes the conservative line, so no harm done so far. I'm pleased the Sanger table is well positioned up front. I have an unobstructed view of tonight's keynote speaker. I don't want to miss a thing.

Oh hell no—I can't believe someone invited

Hillary Montgomery as a guest. There she sits with Michael Dunlap, Lucia Hernandez, John Griffin and his wife, the HR weenie Glenn Hendricks, and Cathy. I shoot a real dagger look at Michael as I greet the table, trying hard not to sound conspicuously insincere. "Good evening, everyone. I'm glad you could make it tonight. This is an important community event, and it's great that we have strong Sanger representation."

I'm sure Michael's liberal self probably invited Hillary. She doesn't belong here at all. I purposely give her a weak handshake without eye contact as I individually greet each person at the table. I should have checked the guest list with Cathy. I would have made sure Hillary was uninvited.

Lucia can't hide the scowl on her face as she gives me a lackluster compliment: "Thanks, Mr. Kelsey, for inviting us to this event. I was just telling Hillary how you have such a heart for this community."

I nod and dare not respond. Hillary doesn't even look my way and begins a conversation with Glenn and Cathy. As they begin serving the meal, I notice her bowing her head for a silent prayer and then excusing herself to the restroom. Don't tell me she's also a bible thumper. As she leaves, I notice she has lost weight and is wearing a very stylish black dress. Maybe Lucia picked it out for her, because the Sanger prized Latina is rocking a fancy red dress. Lucia notices me looking at Hillary and flashes a smile my way. I quickly turn to look at the head table, and there sits the burly cop with a woman next to him who I assume is his wife. She's quite homely looking and most fitting for such a viper. She's smiling enthusiastically and appears to be reveling in her husband's prominence as the toast of the evening. We'll see how long that smile lasts.

When Hillary makes it back to her seat, goofy Glenn pulls her chair out and she thanks him with a wink. I wonder what that's all about. She obviously doesn't know he's gay. She doesn't realize her flirting is totally wasted on a guy who is attracted only to guys. Forget Hillary—I can't let her or anyone else at my table distract me from the real reason I'm here tonight.

As dessert is being served, the mistress of ceremonies stands up to greet everyone. She first acknowledges the sponsors and gives a hearty shout-out to Sanger. She motions for me to stand, but I wave my hand instead and remain seated as the audience erupts in thunderous applause. The last thing I want is for the burly cop to recognize me. Nothing can interfere with tonight's plans.

After acknowledging other, lesser sponsors, she begins her introduction of the speaker of the hour. I almost puke as she describes the burly cop with far too many accolades. "Ladies and gentlemen, it gives me great pleasure to introduce a man who really doesn't need an introduction, because he's so well known in the community and across the region. He tirelessly serves this community in so many ways. It would take most of the evening to list them all.

"He's a committed husband and father who makes God and family key priorities in his life. He's one of the fine police officers working diligently to ensure we live in a safe community. Criminal activity is at an all-time low under his watch. The bad guys don't stand a chance with Officer Nicolas 'Nick' Turner. Nick is a man of integrity and a fantastic role model for all of our Scouts. He achieved the coveted level of Eagle Scout in his early teens. He's been a tremendous mentor to our young men who aspire to meet the same requirements. Let's face it: we all love the man who will deliver our keynote address tonight. Please join me in welcoming to the podium our very own Officer Nick Turner."

The applause is deafening, and the burly cop is sporting one of the widest grins I've ever seen. As he begins to speak, his voice is a bit raspy, as if his throat is dry. The mistress of ceremonies beckons a waiter to bring him a drink. A waiter with a unique mustache responds and hands the burly cop a glass of water, which he quickly drinks.

I give the burly cop credit for his way with words. "Thank you, Carmen, for that very wonderful introduction. I apologize for my temporary gravelly voice. It's undoubtedly the sexiest voice

I've had in years—too bad a glass of water made it disappear." The audience laughs. "It is such an honor to be your speaker tonight. I want to first congratulate the Scouts who received awards and all of our Scouts here tonight with their families and friends. I can't tell you how much it means to me to be a part of one of the finest organizations in our nation—no, the whole world. I also have to thank the men of our community who spend countless hours with our Scouts. Our young boys benefit tremendously from their sacrificial giving and service. Let's give these men a standing ovation. They deserve it."

The audience applauds, and many stand to acknowledge the volunteers.

"Thank you, Mr. Mayor, for coming out tonight with your lovely wife. Please give our honorable mayor a rousing Boy Scout welcome."

The mayor stands as the audience greets him warmly. He waves his hand and points to his smiling wife for acknowledgment.

The burly cop pauses, then continues, "I also want to thank my lovely wife, who willingly shares me with this wonderful community. Stand up, honey." The audience applauds his wife, and she blushes. The burly cop pauses, appears to spend a moment in reflection, and then continues speaking as he puts one hand to his forehead and grasps the podium with the other. It's almost as if he has to control his balance to keep from falling. He shakes his head as a boxer does to recover from a major blow. Then clarity returns to him and he smiles. "I guess I should be totally honest when I speak to you tonight. Does everyone want me to be totally honest?"

The audience yells, "Yes, we do!"

With a noticeable change in his demeanor, the burly cop continues, "Well, honesty it is." He then lifts the microphone from the stand and begins to pace back and forth as he goes on.

"First of all, you should know I really hate this organization and the slimy little rug rats I have to deal with as a Scout mentor. You lousy parents out there want to get them out of your hair at home, so you dump them on me and the assholes working with me. Yes, I said 'assholes.' These guys think they're tough stuff, helping boys become Eagle Scouts, when most of them are pure garbage. They're trying to relive their worthless childhoods through these young boys. All I hear from some of them is, 'I was an Eagle Scout back in the day' or, 'I won this award or that award.' Who in the hell cares? Hell, I cheated all the way to becoming an Eagle Scout. It was a royal waste of my time."

One of the volunteers yells, "Turner, you're a disgrace to the Scouts! Get off the stage!"

The burly cop laughs. "You've got some nerve calling *me* a disgrace. I'll tell everyone what a disgrace is. It's you, watching the boys take showers when we're out camping. Don't think we don't know why you're always offering to help dry some of them off, you sadistic pervert and child molester."

The guy heads toward the stage, but a hotel staffer grabs and restrains him as he yells, "You're a miserable liar! I'll rip your heart out for this. Just you wait!"

The mistress of ceremonies is shifting uneasily in her chair, looking around the room for support or anything to ease her major discomfort and get the now-out-of-control speaker off the stage, but the burly cop is on a roll. "My dear wife loves to tell people how proud she is of my Scout activities. Don't believe a word of it. She hates the fact I'm gone most weekends. I can't believe she doesn't know I volunteer to get away from her fat ass. She is one royal pain in the neck, and I stay with her only because there's no way I'm going to pay her spousal support. God forbid one of the sorry judges I know forces me to pay child support.

"One good thing, Mr. Mayor: I'm glad I have a wonderful woman in my life. You know who the woman is? I'll tell you, you sorry piece of crap. It's your beautiful wife." The mayor and his wife both turn crimson, and she puts her hands to her face. The entire audience is chattering and snickering by now.

Still the burly cop doesn't stop, even though it appears he's now actually trying to. "Mr. Mayor, your lovely wife and I have been getting it on for some time. That woman knows how to love a man. You should hear her talk about your lack of capacity, if you know what I mean. You don't know how to love a woman like a real man—a real man like me, Nick Turner. You might consider getting a surgeon to build up your equipment. Your wife says it doesn't work." The burly cop laughs loudly and points mockingly at the mayor.

The mayor stands up. His wife tries to restrain him, but he pushes her out of the way and makes a mad dash toward the stage. A couple of the hotel staffers grab him and prevent him from reaching it. Many families are now leaving the ballroom with their kids, wearing shocked looks on their faces. The children seem to have been enjoying the unplanned spectacle a little too much.

The burly cop then runs toward the edge of the stage, shouting to the mayor, "Come on up, you sorry sucker. I'll beat you to a pulp like I beat the niggers I love to harass. I love beating niggers, and Lord knows how much I hate the little nigger Scouts. I bet you don't see one of them here tonight. I told their parents this event was only for the Scouts getting awards. I made sure not one of those little nigger Scouts got an award. I don't know why we let them in anyway. We don't let the homosexuals in, and the niggers are worse than them."

The mayor picks up a rod lying near the podium

and throws it toward the stage, just missing the burly cop, who yells, "You sorry bunch of losers. See what I'm talking about? Your mayor can't even through a rod straight, just like his wife said."

Hotel security has given the burly cop some slack, but after his exchange with the mayor, they physically remove him from the stage. However, there's no stopping him—he breaks away from hotel security and rushes back onstage, grabs the microphone, and continues his verbal attack. "Hey, guys, help me off the stage, and let's beat up this piece of crap we call our mayor. I know you guys don't like this miserable runt, so here's the chance you've been waiting for. Let all the idiots out there watch, because they don't like him either."

Someone must have dialed 911, because the police arrive and rush to the stage while the security team leaves. The burly cop's comrades try to settle him down, but he's totally out of control by now. He starts swinging at them as they attempt to restrain him, and he stumbles and falls and starts kicking one of the cops. At this point, they try to distance themselves from their comrade. One of the cops pulls out his Taser and lets the burly cop have it. He screams in pain. "I'm going to get you for this. I'll tell everyone how you're on the take from Thelma's prostitution ring."

Before he can say another word, the cop lets him have it again, for a longer period. This time, the burly cop is in too much pain to continue talking. The officers place him in handcuffs and carry the incapacitated officer out of the ballroom.

People continue leaving in a state of shock. Some of the Boy Scouts and their mothers are in tears. The burly cop's wife is crying uncontrollably. The mayor's wife has already run out of the room as fast as she could. The Sanger table is equally dumbfounded, and I make what I consider the most appropriate comment as I struggle to hide my delight. "This is unbelievable! I never expected this type of madness to happen at a Boy Scouts event. I apologize that you had to experience this insanity. Most of all, I feel sorry for the kids and their parents. I can't believe the garbage coming out of that decadent's mouth. His behavior was reprehensible, and it's a shame he chose tonight to let his real side emerge."

John Griffin is ready to form a lynch mob as we're walking out of the ballroom. "We have to make sure this animal gets the punishment he deserves. Sanger should demand his immediate termination from the police department and have him removed from every position he holds in the community. As far as I'm concerned, this jerk is as good as dead."

It's difficult for me to maintain a somber face, but I play this scene like Liberace on a grand piano. "You're right, John—his tirade was a disgrace to the police department, the community, and the Boy Scouts. Something has to be done so he never again gets the opportunity to engage in such disgraceful behavior." I shake hands with all of the men, nod at the women, except Hillary, and thank everyone for coming.

I can't wait to get into my car and laugh my head off. As soon as I'm in the driver's seat, I pump my fist in jubilation, the way Tiger Woods does when he makes an eagle shot to win a major golf tournament. The burly cop just experienced the Darryl Kelsey form of execution. On this rainy night, he is now dead to this community. He will never recover from tonight's command performance. It was heartwarming to watch him drown in his own words, just as the mud rises to drown me in those horrible nightmares.

As I arrive home, my cell phone rings. It's my main man, Frank Cook. "Hey, my rich friend, how did things go tonight? Did our boy talk up a storm?"

I laugh. "A storm? It was a category five hurricane. I don't know what concoction you used, but it worked to perfection. You should have seen the mayor and his wife. The burly cop's buddies even used a Taser on him. I'm amazed at how you pulled this one off."

In his usual modest and secretive way, Frank offers few details. "The part I enjoyed most was being the waiter with the mustache who gave the dummy a glass of what appeared to be water. You know I don't reveal my secrets, so don't even ask what was in the glass. It took careful planning and perfect execution to first make sure his throat became dry so I could bring him a glass of my favorite water. The concoction makes people speak uncontrollable truths they'd never disclose to anyone, publicly or privately. I just love it when it works. Now you can pay the balance of your account, in honor of a perfect night."

Frank knows I'm anal about timely payments. "Come on, Frank—you'll have the money in your bank account first thing tomorrow morning. You know you've never had to worry about me settling my account."

Frank laughs. "Don't get serious on me, my rich friend. You're the best, and it's always my privilege to make you a satisfied customer. Until next time, enjoy the hell out of this memorable night. We'll talk about the next project in a few days."

I thank Frank and feel the best I've felt in several weeks as we end our call. Sleep creeps into the room, searches for me, and successfully finds me in a way it hasn't done for several weeks. There's no way the burly cop will interrupt my sleep tonight. Maybe there really is a God.

19 LUCIA

The Devil Is in the Details

Last night was one of the craziest nights of my life. I thought *my* family gatherings had a lot of drama. The so-called outstanding police officer dude was totally off his rocker during his weird speech. He was talking as if he had smoked crack or some similarly debilitating drug. On the bright side, it was an entertaining night, if nothing else. I have another meeting this morning with the two *cucarachas* John and Sheryl. They really are like despicable roaches lurking around in the dark and then scattering when the light comes on. They're supposed to provide further details about the project. John had the nerve to speak badly about the crazy guy at the banquet last night, but he's just as obnoxious, maybe more so.

Oh well—even John, Mr. Evil himself, will one day be held accountable for his long list of wrongdoings, and that can't happen soon enough.

As I step into John's office, I say, "Good morning, John and Sheryl."

John gives me his typical phony greeting. "Oh,

good morning, Lucia. One of Sanger's rising stars."
Sheryl just nods and, as usual, lets John do all the
talking. "I'm sorry you had such short meeting
notice again, but we've learned the Castillo project
timeline is much shorter than expected." He glances
over at Sheryl, who is obviously trying hard not to
give away any information with her body language.
"Castillo wants the updated proposal in four weeks,
but we'll need it for review and approval in three
weeks."

I gasp, "Three weeks? That's virtually impos-
sible, especially since I don't even have the team
assembled yet. I have to translate several documents
from Spanish to English before we can really get
started. Can we request more time, given these con-
siderations?"

John shakes his head. "No, that's not possible,
and this project is too important to Sanger's financial
future. We can't ask for an extension, and we can't
fail. If you don't think you can handle the project
within the timeline, we can get someone else to lead
it. I think you know I don't want that to happen. I
know you've been waiting for a high-profile, challenging assignment, and there's no higher-profile
project today in Sanger than pursuit of the Castillo
contract. It could be worth over seven hundred
million dollars just for the first phase."

I regain my composure. "I didn't say I wouldn't
do it. I'm just concerned about the short timeline.

Do you have any idea who can be released to serve on the project team? We need the best possible talent. I would love to have Ernie Morales on the team, because he's the only computer analyst who speaks fluent Spanish and he's also a computer whiz."

John looks over at Sheryl and shakes his head. "Oh, I'm not sure we can release Ernie for this project. He's working another major project."

Sheryl quickly jumps in. "Ernie is also quite new and is still learning the job."

I won't give in to their game playing and speak up for Ernie. "I've heard good things about Ernie, and I need him if I'm going to meet the three-week deadline."

John again looks at Sheryl and shrugs his shoulders. "Okay, you can have Ernie, but no more analysts can be released for this project."

I'm so flabbergasted by these two; I wonder what their definition of "full support" is. I refuse to let them cheat me out of this important opportunity. Come hell or high water, I'm going to take the lead and meet the project deliverables. I begin to speak with confidence. "I'll speak with Michael, and maybe he can identify a couple more people. The translation of the documents, as you're aware, is the most time-consuming part of the project."

John agrees and says, "That's fine, and please let us know if you need our help. I'd like the names of your team by close of business today. Remember, this is a major opportunity and we want you to be successful."

I have to swallow hard to keep from throwing up. Like hell, they want me to be successful. I'll have to get with Michael right away. Oh my God— Hillary speaks fluent Spanish and she's a whiz with computers. I'll make sure she's on the team. She'll have my back with these *cucarachas* who are always up to no good.

As I leave John's office, it takes everything within me to keep my emotions in check. I practically run to Michael's office, and by that point I'm almost in tears. I'm glad he's in and grateful he's alone. "Hi, Michael," I say. "I'm sure you're aware of the Castillo project and my assignment as team lead."

Michael smiles and greets me. "Hi, Lucia. Yes, I'm aware that you are the lead. I'm the one who recommended you for the role. You'll do an excellent job."

Those snakes. How dare they imply my selection as project lead was their decision? I voice my concerns about the tight schedule to Michael. "The deadline for the deliverables is only three weeks away, and John wants my team names by close of business today. I feel like I'm being set up for failure if I don't get the right people on the team. I desperately need your help."

Michael gently grabs my shoulders. "Take a seat,

Lucia. I know this is a tough project, but there's no doubt in my mind you're the right leader for it."

At that point, I can no longer keep my emotions in check and my tears begin to flow. Michael closes the door and gives me a hug. "Hey, Lucia, it's going to be okay. You know I'm not going to let anyone leave you hanging out on a limb. It's not going to happen. Castillo has given us an insane timeline, but it's attainable with the right team. Who do you have so far?"

I respond, "I have only Ernie Morales and myself. The Spanish translations are the biggest hurdle and will take hours to complete."

Without the least hesitation, Michael says, "We'll hire a contractor to come in and handle the translations. That gives the team more time to work on other areas. How many people do you think you need?"

I give his question some thought and say, "It's important to have at least a couple of folks besides me who speak, read, and write Spanish. I was wondering if Hillary could join the team."

Michael looks surprised when I mention Hillary's name. "Hillary? I thought you needed someone fluent in Spanish."

"I do, and Hillary is quite fluent in Spanish."

Michael's eyes light up, as he says. "Wow, I completely forgot Hillary is bilingual. She spoke about her Spanish skills during her initial interview with me. She's doing a great job on another project, with

Rick Segal as her team lead, and even though he's a great guy, I doubt he'll let her go easily. Well, as I think about it, it's probably easier for them to get a replacement for Hillary than for you to find another team member who's fluent in Spanish. Okay, Hillary is yours."

I breathe a sign of relief. "Thanks so much, Michael. I just need the two people from Contracts, Jung Chin and Lillian Brown, who worked on the first Castillo contract, and then we should be fine. Thank God a lot of the work needed for this project was done on the previous contract we lost. Fortunately, I've kept all of the documents."

Michael smiles. "Atta girl. I'll get you the two Contracts folks by this afternoon, and you can have your full team ready to get started tomorrow morning. Anything else you need?"

I'm so happy Michael is such an awesome leader. I answer, "No, I'm good. I don't know what I'd do without you. I really appreciate all you do for me. Is it okay to speak with Hillary about the project team?"

Michael gives a "not so fast" shake of his head and says, "Let me speak with Rick first, and then I'll call you with an update. I think ultimately Rick will be supportive, even if he's sad to see Hillary transferred off his team, and that's more than I can say for some of the other guys, who would go for my jugular for taking one of their good contributors."

We both laugh, and I feel so much better knowing I have Michael's support. In this corporate environment with its dog-eat-dog mentality, he's a breath of fresh air. He recognizes and acknowledges talent regardless of race, gender, physical appearance, or sexual orientation. I just wish there were more leaders like him.

I'm sure Hillary will be excited when she learns she's on my team. My mantra is "This project is going to be a success! This project is going to be a success!" I just have to keep saying it over and over, and after a while, I'll be convinced it's true.

20 DARRYL

Oh, What a Relief It Is

This morning the alarm woke me from the most restful night I've had in weeks. No near-death, mud-swallowing nightmares. I felt absolutely fantastic after my morning run. I couldn't wait to scan the *Daily Herald* to see if there were any exciting local stories. Wouldn't you know it, I found a prominently placed front-page article with the headline "Local Police Officer Arrested for Disorderly Conduct at Boy Scouts Banquet!"

The story read: "At the annual Boy Scouts awards banquet last night, keynote speaker and police officer Nicolas Turner unexpectedly attacked the Scouts, his family, and the community. He began by insulting mayor William Bond and revealing his own affair with the mayor's wife, Susan Bond (an allegation she vehemently denies). The mayor rushed the stage to attack Officer Turner but was restrained by hotel staff. Police officers had to use a Taser on Officer Turner to get him under control. He was then arrested and removed from the premises.

"Turner was released late last night on his own recognizance and is staying at an undisclosed location. Police chief Lemont Nash has been inundated with requests for Turner's termination from the police force. No explanation has been offered for Officer Turner's behavior. Some unnamed sources speculate he may have been using drugs, but a police department–administered drug test revealed no foreign substances in his system. Without a doubt, last night will be an unforgettable night for all attendees, though for the wrong reason. Officer Turner has already received a lifetime ban from the Boy Scouts and was removed today from several local boards. It's safe to say a man who was once lauded for his community service is now viewed as a pariah to the community, and deservedly so after last night's demonstration of his true character."

The article was music to my ears. I quickly completed a transaction through the bank account Frank Cook created to ensure there would be no traceability. Frank doesn't come cheaply, but some things are indeed priceless. The burly cop's suffering is well deserved, considering the emasculation and emotional distress he caused me and, I'm sure, so many other men of color. I feel bad for his wife and children, but not bad enough to regret the action I took. Maybe they'll make amends one day and his family relationship will be restored. This form of public humiliation is a lot worse than death for someone who was so proud of his reputation, which is now in shreds. I can't think of any better punishment. I'll have to periodically follow up on him and see how this plays out.

I can now shift my focus to my upcoming class reunion and work with Frank on another one of his surprise concoctions. In the meantime, I'd better make sure the Castillo contract proposal is successful this time around.

After I get to the office, I ring Cathy to have Michael meet with me as soon as possible. I've got to hear firsthand from Michael about his comfort with Lucia. I'll then meet with him and Lucia together. This contract is too important to have any hiccups.

Cathy pops her head in, "Mr. Kelsey, Michael is available right now. Shall I have him come up?"

"Of course. Please tell him to come up and that he doesn't have to bring anyone else with him."

Michael must have been on his way already, because he pops into the doorway before Cathy can even call him. "Hey, Darryl, what's up?" he says.

"Listen, Michael, I need to know how you feel about Lucia's leading the Castillo project. I've heard good things about her, but is she really ready for such an important project? She has some baggage from the last time she worked on the Castillo contract, and I want to be sure her head is totally in the game."

Without hesitation, Michael says, "Lucia is an outstanding employee and really knows her stuff. I firmly believe we would have landed the Castillo contract the first time if Lucia had been placed in the lead role. She did all of the hard back-room work, and Castillo was very impressed with her results. You may not remember, but you also acknowledged how well she performed. Unfortunately, she wasn't allowed to participate in the final discussions, and everything went south. John and Sheryl made a major mistake, and Lucia had every right to be mad as hell at them. We hear this crap about her accent, and it's bull. No one is more difficult to understand than Henry Barnes; his Deep Southern drawl makes you feel as if you need to go down into his throat and pull out the words."

It's just like Michael the liberal to make this a race issue. "I hope you're not sharing these thoughts with Lucia," I respond. "We don't want to give her any ammunition to take action against Sanger."

Michael's tone shows his displeasure with my remarks. "I'm not crazy, Darryl. As highly as I think of Lucia, I am a loyal Sanger leader, and you of all people know that. Take a look at these project plans she generated last time, which we'll use again this time. You'll see why I'm such a strong advocate for her."

He gives me the plans and continues, "Okay, my main concern is that this time around we get the

Castillo contract award. If you feel Lucia is the right project leader, then so be it. Let's get her in here so I can hear about her new team. She can also answer any of my questions about the project plans. The Castillo team will be here next week, and I want them to leave here knowing they're in good hands. No, in *great* hands."

I don't care if Michael sings Lucia's praises all the way into his retirement; I have my own feelings about her, and they're not as glowing as his. But once he and I review the project plans he gave me, I have no choice but to admit to myself that I'm impressed with her work. Now I'll need to see who's on her team because it's critical we have all the right players.

I buzz Cathy and tell her to call Lucia and let her know I need to see her in my office right away. When Lucia comes in, I ask her to have a seat. "Hi, Lucia, and congratulations on your promotion to project manager. I'm hearing great things about you from Michael."

She flashes her beautiful smile and says, "Thank you, Mr. Kelsey. I'm very excited about this opportunity."

"I'm sure you know how important the Castillo contract is to Sanger. It's a must-win for us."

"Yes, sir, I understand, and I believe we can and will get the contract."

"Great—that's what I want to hear."

"I've reviewed the project plans, and after we make some minor updates, we'll be well on our way. The key issue now is, do you have the right players on your team? Tell me whom you've selected, and why."

Lucia speaks with no hesitation. "Yes, I believe I have the right players. There are five of us. First, I chose Jung Chin and Lillian Brown from Contracts, who played a key role in developing the first Castillo contract. It's important to have fluent Spanish communicators who speak, read, and write Spanish, so I chose Ernie Morales and Hillary Montgomery, who also have strong computer skills."

I'm shocked to hear Hillary's name. "Hillary Montgomery! I thought you wanted fluent Spanish speakers. How does Hillary Montgomery fit into this picture? No way!" Lucia is out of her ever-loving mind. Hillary will *not* be on this project team.

I can see Lucia is not happy with my reaction, as she responds, "Mr. Kelsey, Hillary is fluent in Spanish. She reads, writes, and speaks it fluently. Michael can vouch for her excellent skills and competencies as a computer analyst. We need her desperately, and her current team lead has given the okay for her to work on this project."

I think Lucia has forgotten who's the boss here, and it's not Michael, or Hillary's team lead. "I'm sorry, but we need the best people on this team, and I suggest you get someone besides Hillary."

Michael jumps in: "Lucia, do you mind stepping out for a moment?"

She responds with a sigh of relief. "No, not at all." She leaves the room, closing the door behind her.

Michael looks at me and shakes his head. "What's up with you? Why are you so hard on Hillary? She's extremely smart and talented. She is the best person for this team, just as she was the best person to be your executive assistant. I saw a true racist at last night's dinner, and I'm afraid I'm looking at one right now. You need to get a grip and accept Hillary on the team."

I hate to pull rank on Michael, but he's left me no choice. "Hold on, Michael—remember, you're talking to your boss. You have the audacity to call me a racist? This form of slanderous insubordination could get you fired."

Michael's face turns a bright crimson and he yells, "Well, fire me, then! It's time you were put in check. By the way, right now I'm speaking to you as a friend, not as your subordinate. You're treating one of the kindest and most professional individuals I've seen in some time like she's a piece of garbage. You should be ashamed of yourself. I thought John Griffin was the resident racist and chauvinist, but you've got him beat. What's happening to you, Darryl? You've changed so much, and it's not for the better."

I'm speechless. Michael can't talk to me this way! What does he mean, I've "changed so much"?

He continues in a more civil tone. "I'm your friend, man, always have been. Actually, I'm one of the few friends you have left at Sanger. You strut around like a peacock, with your fine clothes and arrogant manner, like you're better than everyone here. You treat your assistant like she's some little lap dog who's at your beck and call. You speak over and at people, not to or with them. You're not any better than any of us. We're all trying to live our lives to the fullest. At any time, God forbid, we could stumble and fall. I'm telling you something everyone else says behind your back. You're not the Darryl Kelsey I first met, and this new Darryl is such a step down for you."

I can't hold back any longer. "Well, no, I'm not a bleeding-heart, gay liberal like you, if that's what you mean. You go around trying to rescue and bring misfits like Hillary into the company." I regret those words as soon as they leave my mouth, because Michael is fuming.

"Gay liberal who rescues misfits? Thanks for the compliment. First of all, I'm not gay, although I'd be proud of it if I were. You can call me all the names you like, but I just happen to care about people. I would never refer to talented individuals like Hillary as misfits. I have a desire to help the folks who come through these doors be the best they can be. That's more than I can ever say for you! You treat your own people worse than any bigot I've ever encountered. When was the last time you spoke civilly to Jerome in the mail room? People mock the fact that you insist on being called Mr. Darryl Kelsey when all of the other executives are on a first-name basis. Who in the hell do you think you are?"

What's happening here? Michael has always been a friend to me, even when others, like John, shunned me when I was first hired. I had no idea people were talking about me behind my back. I care what Michael thinks, but to hell with the rest of them. "I'm sorry, Michael. I've had a lot going on over the past few months, and I appreciate your being up front with me. I didn't realize I had changed so much, and in such a negative way, as you point out."

Michael responds, "I accept your apology. I didn't mean to come on so strong, but I miss the old Darryl. We'll have to get a drink soon so you can tell me what's going on, but right now, we need to finalize Lucia's team. Are you good with Hillary being on the team?"

He's now backing me into a corner, and I relent only to please him—certainly not for Hillary's benefit. "Yes, I'm okay with her being on the team. But I'm still skeptical of her and will hold you accountable if she screws up in any way."

Michael shakes his head. "Okay, hold me accountable, and I will hold *you* accountable as a team member and a friend to deal with whatever demons are swirling around in your head. Will you call Lucia back and give her your approval?"

I reluctantly buzz Cathy and ask her to send Lucia back in.

When Lucia returns, she looks from me to Michael as if searching for some clue about what decision was made during her absence. Michael breaks the ice by saying, "Lucia, thanks for giving Darryl and me some time to look more deeply into this project before we made a final decision about the right members for the team. As you know, this project is so important that none of us is taking any chances that could lead to a misstep."

Michael looks to me to share my approval of Hillary, and I join the conversation: "After getting a bit more information from Michael, I have no problem with Hillary's joining your team. I must admit, I was surprised to learn Hillary is bilingual. I don't recall those skills being included on her resume."

Lucia doesn't hesitate in saying, "I checked with Glenn in HR, and he was aware that Hillary is bilingual. It wasn't a requirement for the executive assistant or computer analyst position, so Glenn didn't think it was necessary to bring up in her interviews."

There we go with Glenn—the HR gift that

just keeps on giving. I should have known he was involved in this decision. Michael adds, "Hillary shared her fluency in Spanish during our interview, and I was very impressed." I give Michael a *who asked for your two cents?* look. He responds with a sarcastic smile.

Michael must feel the tension forming, because he quickly says, "Darryl, I'm glad we have your approval of the team members. I'll join Lucia in her first meeting with the team to get them properly oriented on the Castillo project. Let's get together in a day or two about that other thing we discussed."

I know Michael is referring to his earlier comment about how much I've supposedly "changed," and I know he's never going to let me get out of discussing it with him, but that doesn't mean I have to look forward to it. So I give Michael a look that cautions him, *Don't push your luck*, and then I say aloud, "Thanks, Michael, and Lucia, thank you for taking on this project. Please feel free to give Cathy a call if you need me to be involved in any way."

Lucia smiles gratefully and says, "Thanks, Mr. Kelsey. I appreciate your support. I know we will achieve positive results this time around. We won't disappoint you. You have my word!"

I can only nod as she and Michael leave my office. I scratch my head, thinking, *What just happened here, and how did I let it happen?* Michael and Lucia have pulled a fast one on me, and now Hillary has wormed her way onto one of the most important projects in the company. I shouldn't have let Michael get away with his comments about my changing in such a negative way. Who is he to pass judgment on me? I am his boss, and I think he forgot that for a moment. One thing's for sure: I need to watch over this project like a hawk watches over its prey. If I don't, who knows what Hillary might do to sabotage Sanger's chances of getting the Castillo contract? I have to keep an eye on that woman and make sure to keep her evil schemes in check.

21 HILLARY

That's What Friends Are For

I am so happy with my job. For the first time in my career, I feel as if my contributions are valued. My supervisors and team appreciate me as a person, not as another expendable, behind-the-scenes employee. I can't thank Lucia enough for encouraging me to apply for a job at Sanger.

I'm caught totally off guard, however, when Rick, my team lead, asks me to come into his office. I wonder why he wants to see me. Since my layoff is still fresh in my mind, I'm a nervous wreck. *God, please don't let someone from HR be in the office with Rick.* He gave me no information about why he needed to meet with me, so my mind is conjuring up all kinds of negative scenarios. Should I call my mother and ask for immediate prayers? I saw Michael Dunlap leave Rick's office about fifteen minutes ago. Rick has told me how pleased the team is with my work, and I've gotten many compliments. *Please, Lord, don't let me lose my job.*

Rick's assistant, Vivian, is all smiles as she greets

me. "Hi, Hillary. Hope you're having a good week. Rick is waiting for you." I smile as best I can, and she winks at me as I walk nervously past her and into Rick's office.

Rick says, "Hi, Hillary. How are you? Is something wrong? You look like you've seen a ghost."

I answer timidly, "No. To be honest, I'm just experiencing a bit of anxiety about this meeting."

Rick gives me a reassuring look and says, "Oh, no, I should have asked Vivian to tell you there's no problem. I need to discuss a new opportunity with you." My heart starts beating faster, and I'm glad when Rick motions for me to take a seat as he explains, "Sanger is pursuing a major contract with Castillo Information Systems, and you've been selected to be on the project team. This is the most important contract Sanger is going after at this time. I had no idea you were fluent in Spanish, but that makes you a hot commodity for this project. Lucia Hernandez, the project leader, spoke very highly of you."

I stifle a smile. I love the fact that even though Lucia and I are still keeping our friendship a secret at work, she's making inroads on my behalf at Sanger. But I feign modesty so Rick won't catch on and reply, "Wow, I don't know what to say. This is awesome. It sounds like a most challenging project. I'd love to work on it, but what about the one I'm currently working on? The team is counting on me to complete the work I've started."

Rick laughs and says, "I must admit, it was hard to lose you to the new team, but winning this contract is Sanger's top priority. You have to understand that folks higher up the ladder than I am had the final say. We will definitely miss you, but they will send someone over to try and fill in for you. I want you to know I'm happy you have this opportunity, even if it means losing you for a while. You deserve every chance you can get."

I am speechless and begin grasping for words. "Thanks, Rick. I love my team, and the opportunity to work on the Castillo project is really exciting. I'll do whatever is needed to help win the contract." I pause for a moment, then say, "Rick, I do have one favor to ask. Please tell me I'll be coming back to your team once this project is complete."

Rick is obviously touched and says, "I certainly hope so. You can count on me to do everything within my power to get you back. Now for the bad news: you will transition to your new team tomorrow morning, so whatever loose ends you can wrap up today will be appreciated."

I can't believe how quickly the transition will occur. "Tomorrow? Whew, that's quick. I'll do everything possible to complete a couple of key items, even if it takes me all night."

Rick shakes his head, "No, I admire this about you, Hillary, but the last thing I want is for you to experience burnout. Just do what you can within reason, okay? I also caution you not to take on too much as you join the new project team. I know you want to show your commitment and value, but just remember, you're worthy of the opportunity and very talented, and at some point you won't have to work yourself to death to prove it."

I understand what Rick is saying, but he's never been a Black male or a Black female with leaders who have low expectations of him when he starts a new position, who thinks he's been selected not for his talent but because someone had to give him the job. How many times have I heard, "Was this an affirmative action opportunity?" So yes, it's now in the fabric of my being to prove I'm a talented and highly competent professional, even though I hate like hell to have to do this repeatedly.

Of course, I won't tell Rick all this. I say simply, "All right. Rick, I can't thank you enough. You're the best boss I've ever had, and I appreciate the opportunities you've given me to use my skills and stretch in so many ways. Can I give you a hug?"

Rick blushes. "Absolutely. Now you go out there and kick butt!"

I give Rick a hug and can tell he's pleased, even though he returns it cautiously. I love this guy.

Vivian gives me a big smile as I leave Rick's office. I guess she knew all along about the opportunity. I can't believe it. Lucia is just too much. There are friends, and then there are true friends.

What a contrast between her and Darryl Kelsey. This "brother" wouldn't give me a chance, and here Lucia not only encouraged me to apply for Sanger employment but now has put me on her special team. Now we *know* God is good. I take a quick break and run to the restroom to text Lucia: *Te amo, mi hermana*. I do love her like a sister, and I thank God for her love and encouragement in return.

I return to my desk and begin the process of completing as many tasks as I can before I join the Castillo project team. Lucia's cell number pops up on my phone, and I'm worried something bad has happened if she's calling me while we're both at work. It's just like me to think the worst. "Hey, girl, what's up?" I answer. "I'm beside myself with joy about being on your team. I know you get tired of my thanking you, but you continue to do so many wonderful things for me, and I'm so grateful."

Lucia replies in almost a whisper, "You deserve everything that comes to you, so stop thanking me. I'm calling about the undercover work we were going to launch to find out the schemes of the evil twins. The new project means we'll have to put those plans on hold. Darryl will have to fend for himself for the time being. All of our time has to be committed to the Castillo project through completion. I know you want to help Darryl, but I think the best help we can give him is a successful Castillo contract. There's no question in my mind John has shifted tactics and is now using this project as a way to harm Darryl's career."

I digest her words and agree. "You're probably right, which is why John appears so eager to support our diverse team. He believes we will fail, but with God's help, we'll show him."

Lucia chuckles and says, "You got it, girl—keep those prayers going like never before. Ask Mother Montgomery to have her entire team of prayer warriors get on their knees."

We both laugh at that, but I'm definitely going to ask my mother to call on God for divine intervention in this project. John Griffin and Jim Waters will not have the last laugh this time. We will have to enlist the aid of heavenly powers that haven't been used to stop those two in the past.

22 LUCIA

Preparing for the Big Meeting

I'm excited about meeting with my new project team this morning. My heart was pounding as I waited outside Darryl's office to see if he would approve Hillary's participation on the team. He was clearly shocked when I said Hillary's name, and I was worried sick he would block her from joining the team. I just don't get that guy. For some reason beyond my comprehension, he appears to hate Hillary with a passion. He didn't know her before, so I guess it must have something to do with a past experience. Who knows what's going on in that arrogant head of his? Anyway, he finally made the right decision, thanks to Michael's strong push for Hillary.

When we talked last night, she was ecstatic about the opportunity to be part of this major project. She must have thanked me a thousand times. She knows this project has to be successful, both for the sake of everyone on the team and even for those who aren't on it. I know some people don't think we'll be successful—especially the two devils,

John and Sheryl—but I'm determined to prove them wrong. Between our work and our prayer warriors, we'll be over the top. Listen to me, sounding like one of Mother Montgomery's disciples. I have to admit, the woman does have a strong connection to heavenly powers, even though she can be nerve-racking at times. No wonder Hillary prays so much for deliverance.

The team comes in bright and early and excited to get started. I explain the project goals and their specific assignments. They are taken aback by the quick turnaround but committed to meeting the deadline. Jung and Lillian are key to completing the required contract changes for the Castillo team visit next week. Ernie and Hillary will work with the temporary translators to ensure the documents are accurately and timely translated. They will also make all the software changes required for the new contract. My highest priority at this stage is to make sure we meet the deadline and are ready for the initial meeting with the Castillo team.

I'm pleased by the team members' eagerness as they accept their assignments, and everything is going smoothly until the devilish duo appears, although I'm beginning to have a slight change of heart about Sheryl. She's definitely not in the same demonic league as John and Jim.

John greets the team with unusual elation. "Hello, team. Are you guys ready to get the show on the road? I'm counting on each of you to make sure we get the Castillo contract."

Leave it to John to come in with his "I'm in charge" attitude. I won't let him make a royal mess of things, the way he did last time, so I speak up immediately. "Hi, John. We just completed the team orientation and are all set with project assignments. I'll let you know if we need your help, but right now, everything is under control."

He totally ignores me and keeps talking to the team. "We can never be too confident with this type of contract. I need a daily update on the team's progress. You folks don't hesitate to call on me or Sheryl for support." He just doesn't get it; he's already trying to undermine my authority in front of the team. It won't work this time.

"Thanks, John. As I said, I'll let you know if we need help. In the meantime, we have lots of work to do on a very tight deadline." I speak directly to the group to let John know the game has changed and a new sheriff is in town. "All right, team—we all know our assignments. Just remember, we are the right people to get the job done. We're team players, we're smart, we're creative, and we're going to get this project over the goal line. Let's make it happen."

The entire group is all smiles as they leave the room, especially Hillary. She winks at me and places her hand over her heart, which is our signal that we're proud of something one of us has done.

John just scowls at me, but I believe I see a look of satisfaction on Sheryl's face, although she's much too intimidated by John ever to show any direct insubordination toward him. As he walks out of the room, he reminds me of his position. "Don't forget, Lucia, I'll lead the meeting when the Castillo team comes next week. You make sure you have all the deliverables ready. By the way, I don't think your team needs to attend the meeting. Sheryl will be there, and I'm sure Darryl and Michael will attend."

I just look at him. He has another thing coming if he thinks I'm not going to bring the team into the meeting. I'm beginning to feel sorry for Sheryl. I can't imagine having to work closely with a chauvinist pig and have him refer to you as his sex slave. God help that poor woman. I don't believe for one minute John's fantasy about Sheryl's being his sex slave. It's a testosterone fairy tale guys like him fabricate to show off to their buddies. He is lying through his teeth to the very gullible Jim Waters. No leader in his right mind would even speak about a sex slave in today's corporate environment—and to think, Jim's in HR. John would have to be crazy to talk about this, even to a weakling like Jim.

Oh well—not my problem. I have too much other work to do to take on Sheryl's issues with that guy.

23 DARRYL

I Haven't Changed That Much!

I'm still mulling over the discussion Michael and I had the other day. Actually, "discussion" is probably much too mild a descriptor—it was more a heated argument. The words he used to describe me are still painful to digest. I don't think even my recent scheme to take down the burly cop makes me quite the person Michael described. He made it seem as if everyone despises me. Yes, I'm proud of my accomplishments and I am better than a lot of people at Sanger. That's just the way it is when the cream rises to the top. I'm not going to change because of petty jealousy from those who don't know how to get ahead. I know people like John can't stand the thought of a smart Black man like me climbing the corporate ladder and achieving significant success. John has a hard time hiding his disgust for me as his boss. He says the word "boss" with as much venom as possible and tries to cover it with a half-assed smile.

It's hard for me to comprehend that Michael thinks I'm a racist. That's coming from a white guy who has never experienced racism. He has some nerve. He doesn't get pulled over by the police just for sport. He hasn't had to drink muddy water on his knees while a burly cop enjoys the humiliation. He doesn't have salespeople follow him as soon as he walks into a department store. He hasn't been denied apartment rentals or home purchases because of the color of his skin. He hasn't been falsely arrested, only to get an apology saying, "Sorry, you're not our guy after all." No one listens to your voice in those situations. I should have reminded Michael of this when he was scolding me.

He's also wrong about Jerome in the mail room. I have spoken to Jerome, but he's so far beneath my level, we have nothing in common to discuss. I've heard Michael asking Jerome about his weekend and the classes he's taking. The reality is, I don't give a crap about what's happening in Jerome's life, and it's not my fault he doesn't have the political savvy or the skills to get out of the mail room. I'm sure he has the appropriate job for his skill level. What does Michael expect me to say to Jerome? There's no reason for me to strike up a conversation with him. In this environment, it's every man for himself. I don't think that makes me a bad guy...so why am I wasting my time thinking about Jerome's plight? Have I really changed as much as Michael described? I decide that while I can't let Michael lay a guilt trip on me, maybe I'll strike up a conversation with Jerome the next time I pass by the mail room.

Michael probably thinks I should help Jerome because we're both Black. It doesn't work that way with me. I had no one to help me; I achieved this level of success through hard work, high intellect, and stellar performance. It's liberals like Michael who make so many Blacks think they're entitled to a helping hand to climb the corporate ladder. That's the damage affirmative action has done to Black people. I'm sick and tired of it, and I will not contribute to its continuation. It's the number-one reason I push the conservative agenda. Clarence Thomas and I are completely aligned in our positions on affirmative action. The last thing I want is for someone to think I reached my current status because I was given a position. I earned it, along with every other role, and I'm proud of it.

Michael was right about one thing: my feelings about Hillary. I'm still convinced she's nothing but trouble, but she's also cunning and smarter than I thought. I think she's up to something I haven't quite figured out yet, but I will. She could even be a plant for a competitor. You never know about some of these sisters. She's probably one of those who will take a mile if you give her an inch. She's been here less than three months, and she's already on a key project team. She has definitely hoodwinked Michael and Lucia for now, but time will tell how well she speaks Spanish when the Castillo team is here and she's expected to communicate fluently with them. I just hope she doesn't embarrass Sanger and cause us to lose this contract. She'll be history if that happens—although maybe that wouldn't be such a bad thing.

No, we have to win the contract. I need to make sure Hillary doesn't attend any Castillo meetings. I'll ask John to tell Lucia her team isn't needed for the Castillo meeting. I can count on him to keep that diverse team out of the room. It's Michael I have to worry about—he'll do anything he can to showcase Lucia, Hillary, and the rest of his little rainbow coalition.

Forget Hillary for now—I'd better call Carol, because the reunion is just around the corner. I need to make sure she's ready. I had the outfits delivered for her to wear to the various activities. But as I dial her number, I'm beginning to wonder if Carol was the right choice as my reunion companion. As a top business strategist and change leader, she almost single-handedly brought her firm back from near bankruptcy to profitability. The girl is wicked smart and knows how to work magic with people and finances, but if she thinks she can change me like she changed her firm, she's crazy. I know she wants me to fall in love with her, but it will never happen, and I'm getting tired of her not-so-subtle advances.

She must recognize my number and feel anxious to connect, because she answers on the first ring. "Hello, Darryl. You must have mental telepathy. I was just thinking about you, and now you're calling. I know you are gifted but didn't know mind reading was one of your gifts."

What a crock. She should save all this gibberish for someone else. "Hi, Carol," I say brusquely. "No, mind reading is not my forte. I'm checking to see if the outfits I selected for you to wear to the reunion were delivered today."

Carol's voice loses its sweetness and takes on a hint of sarcasm. "Yes, Darryl, the outfits arrived today, and yes, they fit perfectly." I have a good mind to tell her to shove it and I'll take someone else. Then she pushes me even further: "By the way, Darryl, I have a sexy little black dress I'd like to substitute for the black dress you purchased. Don't get me wrong, the dress you selected is absolutely gorgeous, but my dress shows off every curve. Is that okay with you?"

I take a deep breath and say, "No, I want you to wear only the outfits I selected. I made that very clear when I extended the invitation. If that's a problem, let me know and I can have the clothes returned, but I need to know now."

I hear Carol's long sigh. "No, Darryl, I don't have

a problem; it's just, you have to see how awesome this dress looks on me."

Here we go again—she really doesn't get it. I don't care about her little black dress. I know she wants to wear it because she's hoping it will lead to some intimate time in bed with me, but she can forget it—she doesn't appeal to me sexually, with or without the dress. So I retort, "Well, I suggest you wear it at another event, because the dress I sent over is perfect for the Saturday-night banquet. I'm counting on you to bring the outfits and accessories I had delivered. Is that understood?"

After a long silence, Carol responds, "Of course. Listen, I have to return a call to my mother, and it's getting to be past her bedtime. I got your e-mail with the travel itinerary, so I'm all set. I'm sure it's going to be a fun time."

I know she's rushing me off the phone. "Good. I'm glad we're on the same page. I'll call you next week and review the final plans. Don't forget I'm having a car service come and take you to the airport. I'll meet you there."

Another sigh, then: "Okay, Darryl. Have a good evening."

I can't believe Carol wants to substitute one of her dresses for the designer outfits my personal shopper selected for her. She'd better be careful, because it's not too late to cancel her travel reservations. I can easily get someone else to join me—

although Carol is a real looker and is going to be the envy of every Black woman at the reunion. That's the sole reason she's going—to attract attention and to get the sisters riled up about her being my guest.

I can see their disgusted looks now. They will definitely be pissed I brought a beautiful, statuesque blonde to the reunion, instead of one of their Black sisters. That's the other reason Carol is going with me. I want to see those sisters drooling when they see today's Darryl. I want them to wish they were by my side, instead of Carol. I can't wait to see the look on Sally Brown's face. She'll hate the day she chose to ridicule me. In fact, they'll *all* wish they had never said those hurtful things about me when we were in high school. I'll never forget the pain and embarrassment they caused me. I live to cause them as much discomfort as I can—especially Charles Watson. I have to make sure Joe has gathered as much information as possible about him. He's my primary target; the others are merely collateral damage. What a happy man I'll be when I make them all squirm.

24 LUCIA

The Castillo Team Visits

My project team has worked like no other team I've ever seen as we prepared for today's Castillo team visit. We've often put in as many as sixteen hours per day, but no one has complained about being tired or overworked, which is most unusual.

When we finished the deliverables for the first meeting, I treated everyone to dinner. We had a fun night, and I'm thankful to be leading such a dynamic, committed, productive, and innovative group. I've learned firsthand from them the value of a diverse team: the ideas and different perspectives from individuals of such different backgrounds add much energy and creativity to solving some of the problems we've encountered.

I've also been amazed by the chemistry that's developed within the group. As you might expect, Hillary is the team's glue, and my girl is showing she's got smarts. I have a surprise in store for Mr. Darryl Kelsey and John Griffin. Word is out that Darryl has told John to make sure Hillary doesn't participate in today's Castillo meeting. He obviously forgot that John couldn't keep a secret if his life depended on it. Plus, he hates Darryl. I can't believe Darryl doesn't see that John is out to destroy him. John is like a venomous snake—everyone except Darryl recognizes him as the most sexist, racist, homophobic leader at Sanger—yet Darryl somehow views him as an ally.

I wouldn't be surprised if John asked me to bring Hillary to the meeting just to aggravate Darryl, but maybe not. The Castillo contract is their stairway to huge bonuses. They all have a rude awakening coming this time if they think my team will be marginalized like the last Castillo project team was. Not this time, Mr. Kelsey and Mr. Griffin. We've worked long, grueling hours together as a team, and we'll present the results as a team. I won't settle for anything less. I know how it feels when someone else gets the visibility and the glory in front of leadership while I get pathetic pats on the back when no one is around.

The Castillo team is already in the executive conference room, so I'd better hurry. My team is positioned to arrive at the appointed time. I will text them ten minutes before I'm scheduled to present.

I walk into the room and see Darryl and John chatting away with Pablo Castillo, chief executive officer for Castillo Information Systems. He sees and recognizes me and greets me with a warm hello in Spanish: "*Buenas tardes*, Señorita Hernandez, *cómo estás?*"

Out of respect for my Sanger leaders, I respond in English. "I'm fine, sir, thank you. It's so good to see you again, Mr. Castillo."

"*Por favor, llámame* Pablo. Señor Castillo *es mi padre.*"

I laugh and translate for John, Michael, and Darryl: "Mr. Castillo says to call him Pablo, instead of Mr. Castillo. Mr. Castillo is his father."

They laugh as if on cue, then introduce me to the other members of the Castillo team. Pablo has brought Jaime Gutierrez, the project manager; Raul Castillo, his brother and operations vice president; and Martin Esteban, chief financial officer. They all speak English quite well, and it's embarrassing that our highly intelligent Sanger senior leaders aren't smart enough or don't have the cultural sensitivity to have taken a crash course in Spanish, if for no other reason than to be minimally conversant with such an important prospective client.

Here we are, getting a second chance with Castillo, but it's still the same old antics. I tried to teach Michael the basics to exchange greetings in Spanish, but, poor thing, he's just not bilingual material. I give him credit for at least trying, which is more than I can say for Darryl or John.

We take our seats around the table, and Darryl

introduces me as the project manager. "Lucia has done an excellent job preparing for today's meeting. Her team has worked diligently to meet all of the deliverables you requested in your statement of work. I'll let Lucia explain things from here. Please let me apologize for a shortcoming of our leadership team—the three of us don't speak Spanish—but Lucia can converse in whichever language you prefer."

Pablo quickly responds, almost with an edge, "We're fine with English; our entire team is multilingual, and we want to make sure the three of you are active participants in the discussion."

I can't tell for sure, but I think Darryl, Michael, and John flush at Pablo's comments. Maybe Darryl's face isn't red, but his chagrin is evident. The Castillo team tries to refrain from smirking but aren't successful in hiding their pleasure over the Sanger team's bilingual impotence. I don't blame them.

When Darryl nods at me to begin my presentation, I start by providing an overview of the key areas of focus to ensure the Castillo team knows their major requests have been addressed. I then announce, "At this time, I'd like to bring in the team that has worked around the clock to meet the Castillo contract requirements. They will provide more detail based on their individual assignments."

Pablo Castillo shows his support by saying, "Oh, yes, please bring in the team," while Darryl shoots

John an *I'm going to kill you* look and they both throw bombshell looks at Michael. John feigns an attempt to get my attention as a show for Darryl, but I totally ignore him. When the team walks into the room, I think Darryl is going to pass out.

I introduce the team members and explain their specific roles on the project. This is one time I don't care what Darryl or anyone else thinks, although I certainly enjoy observing how hard Darryl is working to maintain his cool right now. Meanwhile, John also attempts to look upset, but it comes across to me as just gloating. I think if he believed something would make Darryl look bad, he would be satisfied, even if his own job were in jeopardy. I love Michael for his unwavering support. He's always got his team's back, no matter what the pressure. He gives me an encouraging look and smiles his approval.

As I call on each team member, they all perform at the highest level. I love that each person greets the Castillo team in Spanish, which results in nods of approval from the recipients. But there's no question my girl Hillary is the star. She just shows out. Miss Diva is looking great since she's lost her excess weight. She's also regained her self-confidence since she joined Sanger and began receiving strong encouragement and support from both Rick and Michael. When she saunters to the front of the room to make her presentation, Pablo Castillo whispers to his brother, not as softly as he thinks,

"Mi hermana bastante Negra enciende mi fuego." ("My pretty Black sister lights my fire.")

Hillary hears him and whispers in Spanish as she passes him, "Thank you, sir. I appreciate your compliment."

He almost falls out of his chair as Hillary's response catches him completely off guard. He had no idea that Hillary spoke Spanish beyond the cursory greetings the other team members offered. Word on the street is he enjoys the company of pretty women, and anyone could see he's quite enamored with Hillary. Of course, I don't translate Pablo's or Hillary's comments for the Sanger leaders.

She makes her presentation with confidence, authority, and passion and shows that she clearly understood and has mastered her topic. Pablo decides to test her and requests permission from Sanger leadership to ask his next questions in Spanish. He suggests I provide the English translation for the leadership team. Darryl winces at this request but nods his approval. I think deep down inside, he's hoping Hillary will stumble and stumble badly.

Pablo takes a moment to seemingly reflect on what he's about to throw at Hillary, then suddenly begins speaking Spanish very rapidly, asking Hillary about a major portion of the project within her area of responsibility. My girl keeps nodding her understanding as he speaks. When he finishes, she blows him away with her thoughtful and right-on-point response, speaking Spanish almost as rapidly as he did. I wait to translate Pablo's question until after Hillary responds, thinking Darryl will surely say I helped her understand the question by translating ahead of her.

Hillary takes a seat along the wall after her presentation. Team members would never be granted the opportunity to sit at the table, even if there were enough seats. It's a crazy unwritten rule for some corporations, and a stupid one at that. Darryl seems to be in a state of shock, as if he's just experienced something extraordinary but isn't quite sure how to deal with it. This was not the performance he was expecting from Hillary.

Raul and the other Castillo team members barrage me with questions next. They also direct questions to different members of the team, based on the materials presented for the review. Once they are satisfied with our answers, they nod approvingly to one another and openly voice their satisfaction. Then Pablo speaks for his team. "We're—I think you Americans say—*blown away* by this team's performance. We haven't experienced this level of preparation and knowledge of our systems in some time. Impressive, impressive!" He also makes eye contact with Hillary each time he utters "impressive."

Michael can barely contain his enthusiasm and pride. "We're pleased the team's work meets with your approval. Lucia and this group have done an amazing job, and I can't think of anything else the leadership team can add."

Pablo nods in agreement. "Lucia and her team have more than met our approval—they've exceeded our expectations. I think they would benefit from a firsthand look at the Castillo facilities to close the loose ends in their proposal, which are not very many. We'd like to invite them to spend some time in Cuernavaca, Mexico, to tour our facilities and gain a better understanding of our operations."

Darryl responds, "It's probably good for Lucia and John to visit your facilities. They can then bring back information to share with the rest of the team."

Pablo looks at Darryl as if to say, *Didn't you hear me speak my request in plain English?* He is emphatic when he continues, "I want the working project team only. They've held their own and provided a much better presentation than we experienced during our last visit. We will cover their expenses. I'm making this visit a condition of the contract. Are you okay with my request?"

Darryl is obviously a bit befuddled, but he can't say anything but yes if he wants to land this huge contract, so he replies, "Of course they can travel to Cuernavaca. I just didn't want you to bear any unnecessary travel expenses, with the entire team going."

Pablo smiles as he says, "No problem; these are expenses we will gladly bear in order to have the best outcomes for this project. I have a huge ranch, and, given some of the hotel constraints in the area, I'm inviting the team to stay with me. They will find it most accommodating." I swear I see him smile in Hillary's direction. For some odd reason, I notice that Hillary winces and looks as if she's just seen a ghost when Pablo mentions we can stay at his ranch. I'll have to further explore what's behind that look.

We shake hands with the Castillo team and thank them for their kind feedback. Pablo Castillo is very gracious and quite the gentleman to the end; I believe he holds Hillary's hand longer than the rest of ours as we say good-bye, but it could just be my imagination. Hillary still has that pensive look on her face; I hope everything's okay with her. It's probably due to the very long hours we've all been putting in to prepare for today's meeting. I'll encourage her to go home and get some rest. In fact, I'm going to tell the entire team to do that. We need lots of energy to complete the task ahead. I don't want them to burn out just as the project is getting into full gear.

Michael is complimentary after the Castillo team departs and my project team has returned to their work area. "Lucia, what an amazing job. Your team hit a home run, and I couldn't be more proud of you. I can't find the right words to express our gratitude." John manages a grunt of acknowledgment, but Darryl is the real surprise. "I agree with Michael, Lucia—you and your team were great. I can't believe Hillary speaks such fluent Spanish. I wonder where she learned the language."

I try to hide my joy over Darryl's comments when I respond, "I believe she learned Spanish in college. From what Hillary's shared with me, she loved it so much, she decided to make it her second language." John stares off into some distant world only he knows about, and I thank them and rush back to my new office.

Life is indeed good! What an awesome day—I feel as if I could conquer the world. My dad would be so proud of me. This is one of those times when I would love to talk to him. I would thank him for encouraging me to reach for the stars and always strive to be the best in whatever professional path I choose. I believe he can hear me, so I say aloud, "I've done my best, Daddy, and I appreciate your wise counsel. I love you today as much as I loved you when you held me close as you took your last breath."

25 DARRYL

Revenge Is Near

Carol and I meet at the airport to travel to my hometown of Clifton, Georgia, for the reunion. Our encounter is quite tense as we greet each other in the terminal. It's clear that Carol is still seething over our last phone conversation. I give her a light hug to try and make amends as we proceed to our departure gate, but I think she can see through my superficial gesture.

The flight to Clifton is a real hassle, since it's a small town accessible only by one of those small propeller planes. I am uncomfortable with small planes, especially if there's any kind of turbulence. The South has changed, but the stares from some of the white passengers are like daggers as Carol and I board. I want to yell, *What are you looking at? Haven't you seen a Black man with a white woman before?* There is obviously a shortage of mixed-race couples in this neck of the woods, and I do mean *woods*.

At least our accommodations are nice; when

we arrive at the Clifton Gardens Hotel, I'm pleas-
antly surprised by its quality. There are lots of
people roaming around the hotel lobby, and I
assume they're classmates I no longer recognize and
their families. They look like typical Black people
at school reunions—lots of laughter, pats on the
back, and bear hugs. You can hear them lying to
old classmates about how good they look after all
these years, when they actually look like hell. Black
people have this knack for making each other feel
good in both positive and negative situations, but
for some reason, that knack was never passed on to
me. Maybe it's because no one ever tried to make me
feel good. Why they treated me like crap and made
my life hell, I will never understand. I'll also never
forgive them for how they treated me—never, ever!

All eyes turn as Carol and I walk through the
lobby. I want to make sure they all get a good look
at Carol, so I intentionally pause and look at my
phone, though I'm totally alert to any comments.
Just as I anticipated, the sisters begin whispering all
around us. One woman openly voices her disgust:
"Who is the brother with the white chick? I don't
recognize him, but it seems like he's done well.
Have you noticed how many of our successful Black
men have to parade a white woman around to show
they've made it? It's so sad. They disrespect their
women more than men of any other race. When
you think about it, Black women have suffered

so much to take care of their sorry behinds from slavery to today, and this is the thanks we get."

If Carol is bothered by the looks and comments, she doesn't show it at all and keeps strutting her stuff. That's one thing I like about Carol: she's not easily intimidated. In fact, I think she feeds off this type of adversarial environment. She's walking as if she were on a Ralph Lauren fashion runway in Paris. I enjoy seeing the sisters seething with anger at the sight. They'll experience much more aggravation before this reunion is over.

When we get up to our room, Carol changes into one of the sexy dresses I purchased for her. I admit it looks stunning on her fabulous figure, but I'm still not going to have sex with her. I can't blame her for trying to seduce me, though— who wouldn't want to have a tryst in bed with a handsome Black man like me? This will be the very last time Carol joins me on an overnight trip. She is not happy when she sees two double beds in the room. I know most men would fall all over themselves to have sex with a beautiful woman in their hotel room, but sex is the last thing on my mind as I think about the plans for tomorrow night. I'll play the nice-guy role at tonight's reception and pretend to enjoy reconnecting with this pathetic group.

I've got to find a private space to call Joe to make sure everything goes perfectly at tomorrow's banquet. I go back downstairs and find a nice, secluded area far from the crowded lobby and the rowdy reunion crowd. "Hey buddy," I say when Joe answers. "I'm just checking to see if you have the information Frank will need for tomorrow night."

Joe sounds a bit annoyed when he responds. "I told you I'd have the information, and I've already spoken with Frank. We're both on our A game; all you have to do is show up tomorrow."

I know he's irritated with my constant contact, but nothing can go wrong tomorrow night. "Sounds good. Can't blame a man for checking, right?"

He responds with an acerbic tone. "If you say so, but you've got to trust us to do our jobs. We've come through for you in the past, without a single glitch, on much tougher assignments. I don't see any reason for you to suddenly be concerned. We're looking forward to a big payday, so please chill out, man."

Now *I'm* irritated. "Don't worry about getting paid. I want to make sure everything goes perfectly. Remember, I'm the client and I'm paying the big bucks. So I have every right to make sure everything's going according to plan, with no hiccups. This assignment is a big deal for me, and right at this moment, I'm not ready to chill out."

Joe finally gets the message that I'm not cool with his attitude and backs off. "No problem— we're cool, man. You know we do our best work for you. There's no need to worry. Maybe the three of us can celebrate after this job."

I'm still not pleased with Joe's initial aloofness, so I respond simply, "Yes, we're cool."

After I hang up with Joe, I call Frank. Frank recognizes my number and greets me more enthusiastically than Joe. "Hey, Mr. Big Stuff, don't tell me you've changed your mind about tomorrow night."

"Hell no, I haven't changed my mind. I'm just checking to make sure I can expect flawless execution."

"Have you ever gotten anything less? Man, we're on top of this, and you're going to be pleased like you've been for other jobs. You've got to stop worrying. It's going to give you gray hair."

I'm not worried about gray hair right now; I just want everything to work perfectly. I end the call saying, "You can't imagine how much I'm looking forward to tomorrow night. We'll talk afterward. Thanks, buddy."

After I hang up, I feel relieved and more relaxed than I've felt in a couple of days. Revenge—yes, revenge—is on the near horizon. But then my thoughts suddenly turn to the Castillo contract and the need to make sure that Hillary doesn't make the trip to Mexico, so I decide to quickly call John because I need him to handle the situation for me.

John answers, and I jump right in: "John, this is Darryl. Sorry to bother you, but I need your help. I think it's not a good idea for the full Castillo project team to go to Mexico. The only ones who should go are Lucia, Ernie, and maybe Jung. I don't think it's a good idea for Lillian and Hillary to go. I've heard that Pablo Castillo is a real ladies' man, so we have to be careful about sending female staff members to his ranch. What if something happens to them? Sanger would have major problems."

After a long pause, John responds, "What about Lucia? Aren't you worried about her being at the ranch? I believe she's also a female staff member."

Lucia is my least worry, and I say as much. "Lucia understands the culture, and she definitely knows how to take care of herself. She'd claw his eyes out if he got out of line."

John sighs and responds hesitantly. "You're probably right. The biggest challenge is, how can we send part of the project team without making Pablo Castillo angry and putting the contract in jeopardy? He's made it very clear the project team members are the only invitees. We can't lose that contract."

This guy has obviously forgotten that I'm the boss and I make the decisions. "I need you to ensure only part of the team goes. Is that clear?" I bark.

John sighs as he says, "Yes, Boss, you made it very clear."

Now, that's *more like it.* "Great. We'll talk when I get back to the office on Monday. Enjoy your weekend."

I feel a lot better after I hang up with John. He's a pain in the rear at times, but I can always count on him to get the job done. I understand his concerns about Pablo's reaction if Hillary doesn't make the trip, but John has to also know that I'm the boss and I'm his primary concern, not Pablo Castillo.

I'd better get back to the room so that Carol doesn't get even more peeved with me. As I walk through the lobby, I recognize some familiar faces who eagerly reach out to shake my hand and share lies about how good it is to see me. Yes, they want to see me now that I'm *The* Mr. Darryl Kelsey, a major reunion sponsor with a high-powered job. I want to tell them to go straight to hell, but I greet them warmly and walk briskly to the elevator to avoid unnecessary small talk with these phonies.

26 HILLARY

I'm Scared to Death!

This is the opportunity I've prayed so long for, and here I am, scared to death, instead of celebrating my good fortune. I can't possibly go to Mexico and stay at Mr. Castillo's ranch. When I awoke the morning of the team's presentation, my bed was soaking wet. I thought I had conquered my bed-wetting problem because I haven't had an incident since I started at Sanger. Oh God—what if I have to share a room with Lillian? It will be awful. I'll be the laughing-stock of Sanger if anyone finds out I'm a bed-wetter. I could even lose my job for embarrassing the company. I'll have to fake an illness so I won't have to go. Lucia has commented about how tired I'm looking lately. I've been working those long hours. I'll say I've come down with a viral infection.

Who am I kidding? I can't do this to Lucia. I've often tried to tell her about my problem, because I trust her with my life, but something deep inside has kept me from sharing it with her. She has so much faith in me and has given me the opportunity of a lifetime. No, I can't let her down. I have to tell her the truth: *Lucia, your best friend is an adult bed-wetter.*

I start dialing her cell before I chicken out. She answers almost immediately, "Hey, my sister. How are you? Girl, you hit a home run with your presentation. I'm so proud of you. Just think, Castillo wants us to come to Mexico. How cool is that?"

I take a deep breath. "Lucia, we need to talk."

She picks up on my sadness. "You don't sound like yourself. Something has you down. What's wrong?"

I fight back tears as I say, "Can you stop by my place on your way home?"

Lucia is not having that and says, "I'm coming over right now. Is Mother Montgomery okay? Did someone pass away? Talk to me!"

"Lucia, stop—no one passed away. I just have something important to share with you."

"Okay, I'm on my way. I'll see you in about an hour."

As soon as I hang up, I start thinking I shouldn't have made that call. What if Lucia decides I'm too much of a risk to stay on the project? *Okay, Hillary, stop tormenting yourself with all this negativity. Where is the rock-solid faith you're supposed to have? Everything will work out fine.* I decide to take a hot shower to settle my nerves before Lucia gets here.

Lucia must have been driving like a bat out of

hell, because she arrives in record time. I open the door, and she rushes in, takes off her jacket, and says, "Okay, you're scaring me. What's going on?"

I take another deep breath. "I have to share something with you that I've been hiding for some time. It's so embarrassing that I'm not sure where to start."

I can tell Lucia is getting frustrated with me, as she snaps, "Just say it. I'm your best friend, I'm like a sister, you can tell me anything."

"Okay, I'll have take you back a bit to my childhood. When my father died when I turned thirteen, I had a hard time dealing with the tremendous loss. My mother was very busy with her career and the church, and our quality time together was quite limited. My father took up the slack, and we had a wonderful relationship until the day he passed. He was my rock and the kindest, sweetest man, who loved me unconditionally. You and he would have gotten along great. Anyway, shortly after his death, for some strange reason, I began wetting the bed. My mother thought it was my way of coping with Daddy's death. She kept saying to me, 'This is a temporary issue, and it will stop after a while.' But it didn't stop—in fact, it's continued into my adulthood. It typically happens when I feel stressed about something that will have a big impact on my life.

"My last episode was the night before the Castillo presentation. I was a nervous wreck about the Castillo meeting. I didn't want to let you or the company down. It didn't help that Darryl Kelsey would be there, expecting and probably hoping I would fail. I was too ashamed to tell you this earlier. It's the reason I have the large washer and dryer in my small apartment. I'm so sorry to drop this on you now, but when Mr. Castillo invited the team to Mexico, I nearly fainted. How in the world can I go to the ranch of a key client and wake up to soiled sheets? The last thing I want to do is be an embarrassment to Sanger and cause problems for you or the team."

Lucia looks at me, and then she bursts out laughing. She laughs so hard there are tears in her eyes. I'm like, *This is not the reaction I expected from my best friend. I don't see my situation as a laughing matter.*

After catching her breath, she grabs me by the shoulders and hugs me tightly. "Girl, I thought something was seriously wrong. You had me scared half to death. Please forgive me for laughing—I'm not making light of a problem that's causing you so much pain and distress—but we'll take care of this. The reason I was laughing is that your situation brought back memories of my cousin Miguel. He is this handsome, dynamite man who had the same problem and related triggering events. He found a holistic doctor and got amazing results, with no further symptoms.

"I'm not being mean, but I have to tell you a funny story about Miguel. One time shortly after he began seeing this doctor, he thought he had conquered the problem and fell asleep after a night of wild sex with a married woman he was dating, his boss's wife. He awoke the next morning to her screaming, 'You peed on me! You pathetic slime-ball! You peed on me!' He was absolutely horrified and tried to make it appear as if maybe she was the one who had wet the bed. The good thing for him is, she couldn't tell anyone. His boss was a gangster-type dude and would have killed them both. Of course, the incident ended their affair."

I can't help but laugh when Lucia shares this story, but I'm more interested in the doctor than in her cousin's drama. "So who is the doctor, and is he still actively practicing? When can I see him?"

Lucia laughs again. "Hold on to your panties; he's still practicing, and I'll get you an appointment. You are too funny. Now I know why you tense up whenever I suggest you need to wake up in the arms of a fine brother after a night of killer sex. Hmm."

I can see the wheels turning in her supersmart brain. "Okay, Ms. Sanger Latina Angel, don't go getting any ideas. I need to see this doctor right away. I hope he can fix the problem for me like he did for your cousin Miguel."

Now we both laugh, and Lucia reaches out and gives me another big, reassuring hug. "It's really going to be all right. I've got your back. You can tell me anything. We're sisters, and sisters always support each other. Love you, girl!"

I know she means it, and I say, "I love you, too, and I'm so thankful God put you in my life."

Now Lucia quickly gets back to business. "Okay, so are we good about you going to Mexico? If we can't get you to the doctor in time, I'll make sure we share the same room. Then you can wear those adult diapers. Aren't they called Tepends?" She laughs and I grimace.

"That's not funny, and for your information, they're called Depends. You can't imagine how it feels having to wear those things."

Lucia changes to a more sympathetic tone. "I'm sorry—now is not the time to kid about such things. You know your secret is safe with me and you won't have to be stressed out. Who knows—it may not even be a problem. Of course, you'll have to chase Pablo Castillo out of the room, because he has an appetite for some chocolate candy—and I don't mean See's candy."

We laugh again as Lucia grabs her jacket and pulls out her car keys and then gives me a surprising reminder: "Hillary, your God always takes care of you, so I'm surprised about your anxiety over this problem."

I feel chastised about my lack of faith over this issue. "I'm not sure why, but my prayers haven't been answered on this one. I know God works on his own time, but I don't understand why he's allowed me to suffer with this problem for such a long time."

Lucia smiles as she says, "Well, I guess today marks the beginning of his time and his answer."

We hug before Lucia walks out the door. I thank God for answering my prayers and ask His forgiveness for not trusting Him to deliver me from this problem. I now realize I never really gave the problem over to God and tried to tackle it by myself. Big mistake—I now stand duly corrected. Thank you, Lord!

27 DARRYL

Oh, What a Night!

I've waited so long for this night that now I'm as nervous as hell. Nothing can go wrong with my special plans. I dare not call Joe or Frank, for fear they will say we should forget the whole thing. They might even tell me to jump in the nearby lake and keep my money. I definitely don't want to get on the bad side of these guys. I know what they do well when it's a business deal and wouldn't want to experience their work when they're angry. I'll just be patient and let them do their thing.

Carol started getting ready hours ago. She hasn't been in the best mood all day—actually, since we arrived here. She'll get over it when she gets her check; plus, she gets to keep a couple of very expensive designer outfits. Not bad for two days' work of just looking gorgeous. If she's still sulking afterward, then it's her personal problem.

I'll even give her a glowing compliment because she is rocking the little black dress I selected for her after all, not the one she tried to replace it with.

"Carol, you look amazing!" I gush. "You'll be the envy of every woman in the room, and I'll be the envy of every man. Thanks for coming with me."

She barely mutters her response. "You're welcome. Is it time to go?"

That does it. She picks up her evening bag and heads for the door, never making eye contact with me.

All eyes are on Carol and me as we check in at the banquet reception table and then enter the ballroom. For a bunch of country bumpkins, the room is tastefully decorated with the Goodwin High School colors and an impressive assortment of Goodwin memorabilia. I whisper to Carol, "Don't forget to smile as if you're enjoying being here with me."

She looks at me and smiles convincingly, but something in her eyes tells me she hates being here with me—or just maybe hates *me*. Either scenario makes me feel a bit uneasy, but to hell with Carol. Tonight her thoughts don't matter.

Just then, the reunion chair, Edith Bell, rushes over to greet us. She has obviously tried her best to look elegant but falls short in one of those sale-rack cocktail dresses from a lower-end department store. "Darryl, I hope you and Carol are enjoying yourselves," she says. "You both look stunning. Darryl, I can't thank you enough for your generous support of the reunion. You helped us raise the bar on this event, and everyone says it's the classiest of all the reunions we've held. I'll make sure we acknowledge your support in a very meaningful way. Let me escort you to table number one. We wanted to make sure you have a perfect view of all the activities."

Given the amount of money I donated, I expected nothing less but say, "Thanks, Edith; it was my pleasure."

As we're walking to our table, someone shouts out. "Darryl Kelsey, is it you? My, my, you look amazing." I turn around to see one of my classmates, Yvette Walker, who never said a kind word or even acknowledged me during high school.

"Yes, it's me. Carol, this is Yvette, one of my old classmates." I emphasize the "old."

Yvette recognizes my intention and says, "Hey, don't put too much emphasis on the *old*. Don't forget, we're the same age. It's nice to meet you, Carol. Hope you're enjoying yourself."

Carol doesn't respond verbally—she just nods her head and smiles—so Yvette says, "Well, let me get out of your way so you can be seated. When are you leaving, Darryl? Hope we can catch up before you leave."

Like hell we will. "We're leaving tomorrow around noon, but we already have plans for the morning. Thanks for stopping by."

Yvette gives Carol a nod and says, "Okay, safe travels." *Now* she wants to talk, after all those years of the silent treatment? Hell will freeze over before I'll spend one iota of time with her.

At our table, as I pull Carol's chair out for her, I hear another familiar voice. "Well, I'll be damned— if isn't Darryl Kelsey. It's been ages since I've seen you. How are you, my man?"

I turn to face none other than Charles Watson, my lifelong nemesis. He's still a handsome man, with some graying around his temples.

It's hard to hide my contempt toward him, but I respond politely. "I'm doing great." I think my cool, short response catches him off guard.

"Who's the beautiful lady with you?"

Before I can introduce her, Carol reaches out her hand to Charles. "Hi, I'm Carol, and you are?"

"I'm Charles Watson. I was one of the guys in school that Darryl probably wants to forget, and I can't blame him." Charles looks me right in the eyes as he says this, and I decide to end our awkward interaction.

"Excuse me, but I'm going over to the bar to see if they have Carol's favorite wine."

Charles looks at Carol and shrugs his shoulders as he says, "Okay, man. It's good to see you."

I don't respond as I walk away, but when I reach the bar and begin checking out the wines,

Charles walks up behind me. "Darryl, do you have a moment? I'd like to speak with you in private for just a few minutes."

What does it take for this guy to understand I have no time for him? "I don't want to leave Carol sitting alone." Charles interrupts me and points to my table, where a lovely woman is now sitting with Carol. "Don't worry, my wife has joined her and they're deep in conversation."

I'll give him only a minute of my time. "Okay, but let's make it quick."

Charles smiles and says, "Absolutely. Do you mind stepping out into the hallway, where it's a lot quieter?"

I follow his lead, and when we reach an alcove, Charles turns to me with a very serious look on his face. "Darryl, you have every reason to despise me, and I can see the hatred in your eyes. For years I've agonized over the way I treated you during high school, and I want to say how sorry I am for my behavior—"

I interrupt him to say, "Look, man, that's old news."

Charles doesn't let me finish. "Darryl, it's not old news to me, and it's obviously not really to you, either. I've prayed for this day so I could tell you what an absolute jerk I was, and you need to know why. Please don't take this as an excuse for my behavior, but I want you to know what I was going through at the time. I envied the relationship you had with your father, who was such a good, caring man. You see, my daddy was a sadistic bastard. He beat the crap out of my mother and me. I hated him with all my heart. All I had was the good looks and the phony face I brought to school every day for the crowd. I saw the love you had for your father when he was around and the love he showed you. That's why I made fun of your dad. He was the father I wanted, and since I didn't have him, I played a cruel game of belittling you both.

"I've asked God to forgive me many times over the years, and I just hope you'll find it in your heart to forgive me. I'm not the fool I was back then. I have a wife and two beautiful children I love dearly. The hurt I caused you has just stuck with me, and not a day has gone by when I haven't beaten myself up for being so cruel. I'm asking you, Darryl, to please forgive me."

Charles has tears in his eyes, and I'm speechless. This is not what I was expecting. I don't know how to respond, so I just look at him and walk away.

When I reach the table, Charles's wife introduces herself as Lucy Watson. "You must be Darryl. I've heard so much about you. I feel as if I already know you." She's searching my face for any indication of the outcome of my conversation with Charles but finds none.

I respond politely but with an edge. "I'm pleased

to meet you and hope you're enjoying the reunion. Carol, I think you'll have to come to the bar with me to select your wine. Lucy, please excuse us."

Carol gives me an *I can't stand you* look, then shakes hands with Lucy and says how much she enjoyed chatting with her. As Lucy walks away, Carol looks at me with sheer hatred. "Can't you ever be nice to anyone? You're a rude bastard who treats everyone like dirt, and you know what? It's not worth the money or the designer clothes to stay here with you. I'm outta here! I'll leave the outfits you bought in the room so I have no reminders of you. You are pathetic, and I feel sorry for you. You really need help—I mean psychological help—because you're insane."

Carol hurries toward the ballroom exit and doesn't turn back to acknowledge me in any way. She needs to get over herself! I shouldn't have brought her in the first place. She's a disposable companion I would have dumped anyway, so good riddance.

I return to the table, where a few other people are now seated. I greet them and maintain my cool as the evening progresses. I'm looking forward to Charles's keynote speech. I'll explain to anyone asking that Carol has an upset stomach and had to return to the room to lie down. I'll add she's hopeful about returning but is feeling very queasy. Nothing

and no one will make me leave this banquet—
including an unstable companion.

❀ ❀ ❀

After a delicious meal, Edith goes through all
of the evening acknowledgments. I think she goes
overboard in thanking me for my donation. Of
course, I'm happy everyone now knows I've made
good money and had enough to literally underwrite
the banquet, which is what Edith shares with the
audience. When she asks me to stand and take a
bow, I make every effort to appear humbled by the
standing ovation and thunderous applause.

Afterward, Edith introduces the keynote
speaker, Mr. Charles Watson. The audience also
greets him warmly. It's apparent he is well liked
by all of the attendees, except one—that would be
me—but I join in the applause and smile as Charles
makes his way to the podium. He knows how to get
everyone's attention as he tells a very funny, tasteful
joke. He thanks the reunion committee for asking
him to be the banquet speaker and then recognizes
his wife, Lucy, who is all smiles when he says, "I'd
like the love of my life to stand: Lucy Watson. She's
put up with me for over fifteen years, and I truly
would not have such a fulfilled life without her. I'd
also like to salute the class of 1990 on our twenty-
fifth anniversary. We've all been through ups and

downs on our individual life journeys. I thank God for being with us the entire time. I know he's certainly played a major role in my life."

Charles's voice begins to sound a bit scratchy, and he starts coughing. One of the staff, with a unique mustache, brings him a glass of water and he drinks it quickly. He takes a couple of deep breaths, and his posture changes, as well as his facial expression. Charles looks out into the audience, where everyone is waiting eagerly for him to continue speaking.

Charles clears his throat and shakes his head, just like Officer Turner did at the Boy Scouts banquet, then resumes speaking: "Life is too short for meaningless words, and I don't want to waste your precious time. Do you want me to speak the truth tonight?"

The audience yells out, "Yes, we want the truth!"

Charles responds, "Then truth it is. You probably don't know this, but when I began Goodwin High School, I was a broken kid who used my good looks and athleticism to hide my turbulent life. My father was physically abusive to my mother and me. He once said he wished I had never been born. My mother was fair-skinned, and my father was very dark. I'm sure he thought my light-skinned complexion meant I was not his son, so he never treated me as one. His older brother lived with us, and this wretched man sexually abused me from the ages of ten through fifteen. I'm sure both my mother and father knew, but no one tried to shield or protect me. I hated both my father and mother for not rescuing me from my perverted uncle.

"One day I couldn't take any more and decided to take action. My uncle was a diabetic and took medication to control his blood sugar. I began to empty his medicine bottles and replace the real medication with cheap pills that resembled his real medication from the drugstore. He became sicker and sicker, and one day he died—the happiest day of my life. I did the Michael Jackson moonwalk to celebrate liberation from that despicable creature. But after that, my hatred for my parents, especially my father, only got worse as I grew older. I think my father suspected I had something to do with my uncle's death, although he never said anything to me about it.

"There was one bright spot in my life, and that was the man who collected our trash, Mr. Darryl Kelsey, Sr. Mr. Kelsey was our classmate Darryl's father. He came to our neighborhood twice a week. He was so kind to me and often took the time to engage me in conversation. He was the first adult male who did not abuse or take advantage of me. He was interested enough in me to ask what I wanted out of life. No one had ever cared enough to ask me that, not even my teachers.

"One day, my mother asked Mr. Kelsey, if he

ran across any food items that were still fresh, to please give them to her so she could feed her family. From then on, he'd drop off fresh fruit and vegetables I knew did not come from someone's trash. My mother tried to flirt with Mr. Kelsey to show her gratitude, but he was quick to tell her, 'I have the most wonderful woman in my life, and I wouldn't cheat on her or hurt her for all the gold in Fort Knox. My family means the world to me.' I was so touched by his words, and so was my mother. Here was this kind man who dearly loved his wife and kids, and I had a sorry asshole who hated me for a father.

"That's when I became insanely jealous of Darryl Kelsey, Jr. I decided to make his life miserable at school with constant teasing and bullying. I also got many of you involved in tormenting Darryl. We should all be ashamed. I know I am. For years, I've beaten myself up for my actions toward Darryl and tried to apologize to him today. I don't blame him if he can't forgive me. Please understand, Darryl, I just wanted my father to love me like your father loved you, and that never happened."

Charles begins to cry uncontrollably, and his wife rushes to the stage to try and console him. He can't stop talking and continues with Lucy by his side. "As I think about my mortality, I want to meet God with a clear heart when the time comes for me to leave this earth. I feel better tonight knowing my deep, dark secrets are no longer binding me. Even if Darryl doesn't forgive me, at least I had the opportunity to ask for his forgiveness. Darryl, no child should have to experience the pain you did. I wish you a good life and pray for you every day. I will do so until the day God takes me home."

I am deeply touched by Charles's words, and I know he is speaking from his heart, because the serum in his water causes people to tell their innermost secrets. It's the same serum that worked perfectly with the burly cop, but I never expected Charles's secrets to involve me, especially in this way. I begin to shake, and the next thing I know, I'm also weeping uncontrollably. I haven't cried like this since I was a kid, and I feel arms gently embracing me. I vaguely hear voices saying, "It's all right, Darryl," and "Darryl, I'm so sorry for the pain I caused you. Please forgive me." I can see people on the stage embracing Charles, too. Our classmates have rushed to console both of us with love and tenderness.

One woman puts her arms around me and whispers, "Darryl, please forgive me for the horrible trick I played on you before the senior prom. Like Charles, I've been angry at myself for years for doing that. My nastiness was inexcusable. Please forgive me."

I look up and see an older but still beautiful Sally

Brown. I am too choked up to speak and only nod my forgiveness. When I finally regain my composure, I get up from the table, walk up to the stage, where Lucy is still holding Charles, put my arms around him, and whisper, "I forgive you, and I'm sorry for everything we both suffered." We embrace for what seems like hours. I don't think there's a dry eye in the ballroom; even staff are wiping their eyes.

Lucy hugs me and thanks me for releasing her husband from his agony. "Darryl, you'll never know how much your forgiveness means to Charles. He's been shackled with guilt for so many years because of the pain he caused you, and now he's free to take the next step in his life's journey. Thank you, Darryl."

There is no discussion after that. Edith returns to the podium and says the reunion awards—who traveled the farthest, who has the most children/grandchildren, and so on—will be shipped to deserving individuals. She asks each of us to fully embrace this time of healing. She thanks Charles for being so open and sharing truths none of us was ever aware of at school, given his charming, cheerful personality. She thanks me for giving Charles the gift of forgiveness.

Edith then says something to the audience that gains my utmost respect. "To all of you here tonight, we saw one of our own share about his childhood pain and lasting guilt." She turns to Charles.

"Charles, we love you dearly. You are truly a man of honor, and God bless you for having the courage to be so vulnerable in such a public forum." She faces the audience again and says, "I don't know about you, but some of the words Charles shared about his uncle weren't clear to me. I'm sure we all feel badly this horrible man, Charles's uncle, died from diabetes. That's what I heard Charles say, and I'm sure if any of us were asked, we'd all have different versions of Charles's words. There is one thing we all heard with absolute clarity in regard to his uncle: the man's diabetes was the cause of his death."

There's a resounding "Yes, that's what I heard" throughout the room. Edith thanks everyone and then walks over to the videographer who is taping the speech and asks for the DVD. She takes the disc with her, and I'm sure no one will ever have the opportunity to hear or view Charles's recorded speech.

I feel drained and head to my room to engage in some serious self-reflection. My cell phone rings as I walk in, and the caller ID says it's Frank. "Hey, my rich friend, how did things go tonight? I bet the bastard talked up a storm and embarrassed the hell out of himself."

I take a deep breath and say, "Yes, he's a changed man in more ways than one. As always, the concoction worked to perfection."

Frank chuckles and says, "I aim to please one

of my best customers. Looking forward to the next project. Sweet dreams."

After he hangs up, I sit on the bed and a million thoughts race through my head. Have I really become a monster shrouded in hatred? Carol literally threw the purchased designer outfits across the bed before leaving the hotel. They surround me now and appeared to be mocking me in her absence. She thinks I'm an awful human being, and maybe she's right. *Am* I the person Michael described in our disagreement over Hillary's participation on Lucia's team? The answer doesn't come soon enough, as I fall into a deep slumber.

28 HILLARY

Am I Really Going to Be Cured?

When I wake this morning, my eyes eagerly greet the bright sun as its rays creep through my bedroom window, leaving an array of colors in its path. For the first time in years, I am hopeful my embarrassing problem will soon come to an end. What would I do without Lucia? I wish I had told her about the problem much sooner, but I was too ashamed. How do you tell your best friend you are still a bed-wetter at twenty-six years old? The opportunity to meet with Dr. Franco Bellamy is truly an answered prayer. Lucia has connections galore and was able to get me in to see Dr. Bellamy in one week, compared with the typical eight-week wait others are currently experiencing.

I was fretting myself into a tizzy about making the trip to Mexico if my problem wasn't under control, and I had come up with a dozen excuses for not going before my talk with Lucia, but now I can hardly contain my excitement about this travel opportunity. I can still see the look of surprise on the Castillo team's and Sanger leaders' faces when they heard me speak fluent Spanish. I had hoped my Spanish fluency would someday lead to the perfect job opportunity, but who knew it would happen so quickly? It's amazing how everyone is so blown away when a non-Hispanic Black woman from Georgia speaks fluent Spanish.

I've always been amazed when some of my white colleagues have "complimented" me by saying, "Hillary, you are so articulate!" As if, as a Black woman, I'm speaking a foreign language when I use proper English. One idiot I worked with a while back had the nerve to ask me where I learned to speak English so well. He deserved my sarcastic response: "Well, you know, it started with 'Dada' and then progressed to 'Mama' when I could make the harder consonant sounds. At about two years old, I was speaking complete sentences."

He looked at me as if my response had insulted him. "Wow, aren't we touchy? I was giving you a compliment."

I quickly chided him for his error in judgment. "No, you were insulting me. Don't ever ask a Black person or anyone born and raised in America such a stupid question."

The guy later shared with my supervisor in a supposedly casual conversation that I had a chip on my shoulder and insulted him after he gave me a compliment. Worse still, my supervisor raised the issue during my annual performance evaluation. I loved how she wove it into my development needs. "Hillary, it's a good practice to show humility and graciousness when someone gives you a compliment. One of your colleagues commented on how you nearly bit his head off when he complimented you about your articulate speech. You have such potential, and we don't want people thinking you have a chip on your shoulder."

I immediately started praying before responding to her and asked God to take control of my tongue. It's not easy defending yourself to your supervisor when you were the one insulted by your colleague. He should be the one explaining his actions and being held accountable for his insulting comment. But, as usual, I put aside my emotions and responded with the utmost professionalism. "I've had only one colleague who would think his insulting comment was a compliment, and I'm sure we both know who he is. Believe me, it's not a compliment to tell an American-born Black person she is very articulate because she speaks English well. We are not foreigners; we learn English during early childhood, just like other Americans. I'm sorry, but I can't smile and say thank you when someone insults me, especially when it's racially demeaning. Perhaps I'm misunderstanding you, but is that what you're asking me to do?"

She flushed and said, "Of course not. I wasn't aware such a comment was offensive to Blacks, so I apologize for my own ignorance."

Her response was better than what I'd expected, and I give her credit for being honest. The sad thing is, many supervisors lack the ability or the willingness to admit their ignorance around racially offensive conduct. Employees of color are often penalized for their reactions to this kind of racist behavior in the workplace. I know many Blacks, in particular, who are given lower performance ratings or denied promotion opportunities because a white peer or supervisor thinks they have the deadly "chip on their shoulder."

I try to purge my mind of those incidents as I lie here this morning, because they only cause anger and frustration. *Okay, Hillary, get your mind back on something you've been waiting to have happen for years. You're going to be cured of your bed wetting by Dr. Franco Bellamy.*

Lucia arrives at eight thirty to drive me to my nine o'clock appointment. Dr. Bellamy's receptionist greets her with much fondness. After filling out the required paperwork and making sure I have insurance coverage, I'm placed in an examination room to wait for Dr. Bellamy. He has all kinds of certificates and diplomas on the wall, so he must have his act together. After about ten minutes, in walks the most handsome man I've ever laid eyes on. Just seeing him is enough to make me pee on myself. He takes my hand and looks directly at me with eyes the color of the deep blue sea. "Hillary, how nice to see you. I'm Dr. Franco Bellamy. Lucia has shared lots of good things about you. I understand you have a little problem."

I'm glad I'm sitting, because I would probably melt onto the floor otherwise. I'm surprised when I open my mouth to speak that a bunch of gibberish doesn't pour out. Instead, I hear myself sounding more composed than I feel inside, saying, "Nice to meet you, Dr. Bellamy. I have a big problem with my bladder at night, especially when I'm experiencing a stressful situation. It's an embarrassing problem to be a bed-wetter at twenty-six years old. I've tried everything possible to get rid of it, including multiple specialist visits, with no success."

Dr. Bellamy has a tender but somewhat direct manner. "I understand, and it won't make you feel any better, but this problem is more common than you think. Tell me more about when it started and the medical or psychological treatments you've had in the past."

After I share all the treatments I've had and the fact that none of them has corrected or controlled the problem, Dr. Bellamy gets right to the point: "I imagine you're probably thinking, *What can one more doctor do differently to solve the problem?*"

I can think of a few things he could do to make

me forget the problem, but I'm a Christian woman and won't share those with him. "Dr. Bellamy, I will be grateful if you can help me either eliminate this problem or bring it under control. I'm too embarrassed to date, and my quality of life has suffered far too long. Who wants to date a twenty-six-year-old woman who wets the bed?"

Dr. Bellamy tries to offer some reassurance. "I believe we can fix the problem. You'll be happy to know so far I have a great track record with cases like yours. I'm optimistic about a treatment plan for you. I know it's hard after so many years, but I want you to be optimistic as well."

I have to hold back my tears as I say, "My optimism left me many years ago, but I will work hard to regain it. How soon will I begin treatment, and how long will it take before I see good results?"

Dr. Bellamy smiles, and those blue eyes twinkle when he says, "We began treatment when you agreed to regain your optimism. We'll need to get some lab work and rule out any physical factors. It takes about three to four days for the lab results, so we'll schedule your next appointment in about five days."

I'm getting anxious because my trip to Mexico is just around the corner, so I ask, "We're going on a business trip to Mexico in two weeks. Is it possible for me to see some results by then?"

Dr. Bellamy responds, "There is no overnight

cure. We have to get a handle on what's causing the problem and then work toward the best treatment plan. It could take three to four months before you see improvement. I've had only one patient with a two-week improvement, and we discovered a bladder issue, which was easily fixed. From what you've shared, I don't think you have a bladder problem, but I won't know until we get the lab results."

My tears begin to fall, and Dr. Bellamy puts an arm around my shoulder. "Hillary, we're going to fix the problem, but you'll have to be patient. We're going to have to work on how you handle stress as part of the treatment. I believe that alone will be helpful to you. Remember the optimism you're regaining. It's going to be okay. Make an appointment with my receptionist for the lab work and your next visit."

I find myself hoping he'll kiss me to make me feel better, but I know I must be hallucinating for a moment. Instead, Dr. Bellamy squeezes my shoulder, as an adult does to comfort a child, and shakes my hand as he gives me the paperwork for the lab work.

Lucia is very encouraging on the way back to my apartment, and I'm beginning to feel hopeful that I might be finding a real cure. She reminds me that she will be my roommate in Mexico, and we'll have a perfect plan to make sure no one finds out about my problem. "Who knows?" she says. "Maybe you won't even wet the bed because you'll be with me, your best friend. Hey, maybe I can wake you every two hours to use the potty, like my mother did for me when I was a kid."

I respond sarcastically. "Thanks, Lucia. Such thoughtfulness really warms my heart. Then we'll both fall asleep during the Castillo meetings, and Mr. Darryl Kelsey will meet us with pink slips when we return from Mexico." As we laugh, I feel blessed to have such a wonderful and loving friend who makes me see the humor in things even when she insults me. It's just like Lucia to say exactly what I need to put me at ease.

29 DARRYL

It's Time for a Change

After I arrive home from the reunion, I take an additional day off from work to engage in deep self-reflection. Am I really a monster? Have I let my childhood experiences shape the man I've become? Why do I hate so deeply? Why is revenge a must for me whenever I'm wronged? Why does the revenge have to be so devastating to the person who wronged me, like the burly cop? Why do I treat women, especially Black women, the way I do? I feel badly about the way I treated Carol. She had every right to walk out on me. Why have I been so awful to Hillary? She hasn't done a thing to me, yet I've treated her like dirt. The truth is, she reminds me of the girls in my class who laughed at me and joined the others in making my life miserable. I've had a thing against Black women ever since. I've got to talk with Michael. I trust him, and I know he'll keep in confidence everything I share with him.

I dial Michael's cell, and he answers. "Hi, Michael. This is Darryl."

"Hi, Darryl. I know it's you. Remember, you're on my caller ID. What's up, man?"

In spite of my best efforts to control my emotions, I become choked up. "I need to talk with you. Do you have time this evening to meet for a drink?"

Michael sounds worried when he says, "Sure, man—is something wrong? You don't sound like yourself. Do I need to come over now?"

I respond, "No, that's not necessary; I'll tell you about everything when we meet. How about Mike's Bar at six o'clock?"

"That's fine," he says. "I'll meet you there."

After I hang up, I decide to call Carol and apologize. Her phone rings and rings, and it goes to voice mail when she doesn't answer. I know she knows it's me, because she also has me on caller ID. I decide not to leave a message and will apologize in person as soon as I can, if she'll even meet with me.

Just then, my cell rings and it's Lucy Watson. When I accept the call, her voice is trembling on the other end. "Hi, Darryl. I'm sorry to bother you, but I wanted you to know that Charles passed away this morning."

My heart beings to pound, and I say, "Oh my God. I hope it's not because of anything I've done."

"No, Darryl, Charles has been ill for some time, and one of his final wishes was to make things right with you. I want to thank you for offering your forgiveness. It allowed him to die peacefully, without the guilt he's suffered for so many years. He asked me to call you and let you know how much he appreciated your forgiveness. Did you get the letter Charles sent you?"

My tears begin to fall as I absorb Lucy's words. "I haven't checked my mail since I returned, but the letter is probably in my mailbox. I'll check it right away. Lucy, I'm so sorry for your loss. I regret Charles and I didn't get a chance to connect sooner."

Lucy speaks consoling words. "You know, Darryl, the reunion was as perfect a time as any. Everything works in God's own time. I'm glad I got to meet you, and I hope we stay in touch. By the way, you should know Charles named our third son Darryl. I would love for you to meet him. He's a junior at the University of Arizona and an honor student."

I'm now weeping and unable to speak coherently, but I stammer, "Lucy, I'm so sorry, I'm so sorry."

She tries to console me again. "It's okay, Darryl. Charles was at total peace with your gift of forgiveness."

My voice is barely above a whisper as I ask, "Will you please let me know when the funeral arrangements are final? I'd like to attend."

"That won't be necessary. Charles was very

clear he wanted no fanfare after his death. He had a great life, and I promised him his ashes would be scattered over the Pacific. The children and I will celebrate this wonderful man who made our lives complete exactly as he asked. Take care of yourself, Darryl."

I weakly respond, "You do the same, Lucy. Good-bye."

I throw myself across the bed and bury my head into my pillow. Self-loathing overcomes me to the extent that I can barely breathe. I'm a poor excuse for a man. I have allowed my years of bitterness and anguish to drive the pain I've caused so many others. I don't like Mr. Darryl Kelsey. I hate who he's become, and I know it's time to change. I silently pray: *If there's a God, please help me. I need your help, and I need it now.*

I must have fallen asleep, because the next thing I'm aware of is a banging at the front door. It's Michael, yelling, "Darryl, are you in there? Darryl, answer the door!"

"Okay, okay, I'm coming."

When I open the door, Michael is clearly alarmed. "Man, don't scare me like this. First you call me, sounding upset, saying you need to talk, and then you don't show up at Mike's. What's up? You look like hell. What's wrong?"

"Michael, I'm a total mess. You said I had changed for the worse and people don't like me. I don't know who or what I've become. I just know I don't want to be the person I am right now."

Michael tries to back off his earlier comments. "Hold up—there was a lot going on that day with the Castillo contract deadline facing us. I probably said things in my eagerness to get the project under way. You can't take seriously everything I said during the heat of the moment."

I shake my head. "No, you were right. I can see how people avoid me, on the elevator, walking through the halls, in the parking lot. You called me a racist and a chauvinist pig and compared me to John. I appreciate your being my friend and for being honest with me. I've become a driven freak, and it's not who I want to be."

Michael again tries to make me feel better. "Look, man, you're not a freak. Yes, you've changed, and it's clear something in your personal life has led to this change. I'm your friend, and maybe you need to get professional help to sort things out."

"Great, now you think I'm crazy. I can't go for counseling—what will people think of my going to a shrink?"

Michael waves off my concern. "I never said you were crazy, Darryl; there's absolutely no shame in seeking help. And to hell with what people think! You've been living your life to get approval or recognition from others, and it's time to let it go. You need a fresh start with someone who can help you deal with those demons in your head. I had to get help at one point in my life. It was the best decision I could have made for my mental and physical health. Would you go get treatment if you had pneumonia?"

I don't know why he's making this odd comparison. "Of course I would get treatment, but this problem is different."

"No, it's not different—look at you now. You're a mess, and your mind and body are crying out for help. Take the time now to get well, and no one has to know your personal business unless you tell them. I certainly won't tell anyone."

I sit down and put my head in my hands. "I don't even know how to go about getting help."

Michael speaks with such kindness. "Don't worry, I know a fantastic guy who I think is perfect for you. If you like, I can connect you with him. Hell, I'll even go with you to your first appointment."

It takes me a minute to absorb the kind of friendship Michael is showing me. I've never had a friend like him, and I've taken his kindness for granted for too many years. "Thanks, Michael. I can't thank you enough for being here when I needed someone to talk to."

"Don't thank me; just get the help you need. Have you eaten today?"

"As a matter of fact, I haven't."

"Okay, I've got to run a quick errand across town. Why don't you meet me at Sarah's Cafe in an hour, and we'll grab a bite to eat?"

"Sounds good. I'm starving." We shake hands and then embrace as Michael leaves. I feel a tremendous sense of relief and gratitude for the most genuine demonstration of caring I've ever experienced.

I realize I still haven't checked my mailbox since Lucy's call. When I go outside to check the contents, I discover an envelope addressed to me with Charles's return address. I go back inside and lie across the bed and begin to read the letter.

Dear Darryl,

It was good to see you at the reunion. You look fantastic, and it was great to see you're experiencing much prosperity. Thank you for your tremendous sponsorship of the reunion. It was special in so many ways.

I want to thank you for the very special gift of forgiveness you gave me at the reunion banquet. I was beginning to doubt your forgiveness was possible, given our brief exchange shortly after you and your guest entered the ballroom. I could see the pain and the contempt all over your face when you turned around after hearing my voice.

What a night it was for me. When I got up to give my speech, I was prepared to give one talk and ended up doing something totally different. I'm not sure what came over me, but maybe it was the potent Georgia water. Remember the old wives' tale about its powers? I had no idea I would share the things in my life that have been tucked away in the recesses of my inner being for so many years. I can only say what a cleansing experience it was to finally share those things. It was if Jesus himself came down and lifted away all of my guilt and pain to prepare me to meet him.

I'm not sure if I'll be on this earth when you read this letter. I was so overcome with emotion, I didn't get to tell everyone about my terminal illness. I couldn't escape the curse of cancer and have only a short time left. My friends look at me and say I look great and my recovery is going well. It makes me feel good to hear those kind words, but I have tremendous suffering internally. I guess I've always put up a great front, just like in high school.

I didn't write this letter to talk about my imminent demise, though. When I saw the hatred and pain on your face, I didn't want to leave this earth without telling you to give yourself the gift of letting go of the past. You couldn't see the cancer eating away at my body, but I could see the hatred eating away at yours. Life is too precious and too short to waste it on anger and revenge. You have a great life ahead of you, and it's time for you to live it. I could see the discomfort in your guest's face and now understand that the hatred in your heart had spread to hers. Do you want hatred and bitterness to be your legacy?

You're probably thinking, who am I to tell you how to live your life, since I'm the source of much of your bitterness? I've always wanted to do something special for you to make amends for the past. After seeing you at the reunion, I now know there's nothing more precious to give you than the gift of honest feedback. Please accept this gift as I gladly accepted your gift of forgiveness. Darryl, please let go of your anger, your hatred for others who have hurt you, and, most of all, your self-hatred. Allow joy to enter the crevices of your heart and envelop you.

Know that I love you and you can't do anything about it. I pray God's continued blessings in your life. I hope you get to know my wonderful family. Lucy is awesome, and my sons are the best. I especially want you to meet my son Darryl. That young man is going places, just like his namesake.

Darryl, this is my farewell. I hope the afterlife allows me to monitor your progress. I go in peace.

Your friend,
Charles Watson

My tears are falling uncontrollably now. It's as if Charles sent his letter to start the process of washing away my pain. I wish I'd read it before he passed away. I would have let him know I accept his gift of honest feedback and will take to heart his wise counsel. I've longed to feel peace and joy all my life. I didn't realize the dam of hatred I'd built in my heart had kept both peace and joy captive. I can feel the dam beginning to crumble away, and it's a great feeling. I'll get the help Michael suggested to totally remove it.

30 LUCIA

Mexico, Here We Come!

Our team's excitement about the trip to Mexico is through the ozone layer. I had to pinch myself as I left home for the airport this morning. I can still hear my mother's words as she hugged me good-bye. "Lucia, I can't believe you're leading a Sanger team headed to Mexico. My sweet girl, you have finally arrived. I'm so proud of you. Your daddy is smiling down from heaven. You go to Cuernavaca and make the best of this great opportunity."

I can feel Daddy's presence in my heart. He was such a good man. This *is* the opportunity of a lifetime, and I aim to make the best of it.

I arrive at the airport and check in for my international flight. As I walk to my departure gate, my team is sitting there already. Their faces are glowing with excitement as we exchange greetings. I see that Hillary has saved me a seat next to hers, and she beams at me as I sit down. I'm happy she's feeling much better. Her second appointment with Dr. Bellamy went quite well. After reviewing the lab results, he thinks he's isolated the cause of Hillary's bed wetting and, thank goodness, it's not a physical problem. It's all in my girl's head. Stress and anxiety are triggers for the bed wetting, and it's directly linked to the death of her father. I can't believe she's harbored this secret all these years I've known her. I always asked her about the oversize washer and dryer, and I've been satisfied with her response that doing the largest possible loads of laundry reduces her electric bill. I think she missed her calling as a counterintelligence agent. The girl can definitely keep a secret. I'm glad she's finally shared her biggest one with me and is more comfortable about going to Mexico as a result, especially since we'll be rooming together. Bless her heart for carrying such a burden. She knows her secret is totally safe with me.

It's hard to believe Sanger's number-one devil, John Griffin, kept trying to accompany us on this trip. Thanks to Pablo Castillo for quickly squashing those attempts. Pablo made it clear he wanted only the working team to make the visit. I'm so happy, because I know John, the venomous snake, would be up to no good. What surprised me most of all was Darryl's reaction to John's not accompanying the team. Usually he's pushing for John to go so he can spy on our every move and report back to Darryl. I'm not sure what it is, but there's something going on with Darryl. He hasn't been his usual arrogant and snobby self. He's been much more subdued, but not in a way that makes him look as if he's plotting his next move. If I weren't so suspicious of him, I'd say he looks almost peaceful. One day I saw him at the second-floor Starbucks, getting his own latte. He smiled at me, and I was so blown away, I almost fainted.

Hillary snaps me out of my reverie by nudging me and saying, "It's time to board." Our seats on the plane are next to each other, and Hillary leans over and speaks just above a whisper to make sure no one else hears our conversation: "I can't believe I'm traveling to Mexico on business. My mother has told all of her friends about my international travel. Of course, she voiced a gazillion concerns about my safety. The cartels are so active, and women like us are kidnapped every day. She even suggested the Castillo brothers were members of a cartel and are using their business as a facade to lure you, Lillian, and me to Mexico and sell us as sex slaves. They will then murder Ernie and Jung."

Mother Montgomery stories always make me laugh. "Girl, I think I know why you started wetting the bed as a teenager. You know I love Mother Montgomery, but she should be writing murder mysteries. What an imagination."

Hillary good-humoredly speaks about that wonderful mother of hers. "She means well. My mother has always been a worrier, which is why she prays all the time. She has a knack for turning the most positive event into something very ominous. She made me promise to call her at a specific time each day. She said she would alert the authorities if I failed to call. I told her I would call her once a day, and that's it. If she calls anyone, I won't speak to her again."

We both laugh, and I ask a rhetorical question: "Do you really think the silent treatment will work with her?"

Hillary says, "No, God bless her soul, she has every member of her church praying for our safety, which is a good thing."

I agree—we can't have enough of her prayers.

After eight hours of air travel, we finally land in Mexico City. We spot a guy holding a sign reading SANGER TEAM and eagerly walk toward him. I introduce him to everyone in Spanish.

He responds in English. "Welcome to Mexico! I am Enrique, and I'm here to assist you with your baggage and transport you to the Castillo ranch in Cuernavaca." We gather our things, he loads our bags into a large van with the help of airport staff, and then we're on our way.

Enrique tells us it will take about an hour to get to the ranch. I notice there's another brawny-looking guy in the front seat of the van with Enrique; he isn't introduced to us, but I hear Enrique call him Carlos. Carlos watches every move anyone makes toward the vehicle, and I'm sure both he and Enrique are fully armed. His presence gives me chills, but as it gets darker, I'm glad he's with us. I also have a greater sense of gratitude that Mother Montgomery is praying for our safety.

We arrive at the ranch, and it looks more like an elegant hotel than any ranch I've ever seen. The place is sprawled over at least a hundred acres. You'd think we were arriving at the strip in Las Vegas, there are so many huge floodlights everywhere. A mariachi band greets us with lively music, and Pablo Castillo is standing at the massive wrought iron gates to greet us. He and the members of his team all welcome us. My imagination may be playing tricks on me, but he seems to hold on to Hillary a bit longer when he hugs each of us. I'm a bit surprised that he's so physically affectionate with all of us right off the bat, but I have to admit, it's nice to be greeted so warmly, when usually all I get is a stiff handshake in these kinds of business exchanges.

The ranch workers grab our bags, and Pablo directs them to show us to our rooms. "Please freshen up and come back to enjoy the feast we have prepared for you." I'm so tired, I just want to get to bed, but I know we have to accept this warm hospitality. Hillary and I are shown to a fabulous suite—actually, more like a penthouse. We enter the sitting room to see two matching sofas and the most elegant window coverings. Original Mexican paintings line the walls. As we walk into the bedroom, there are two plush king beds with beautiful comforters and matching draperies. In a smaller sitting area are two overstuffed chairs and ottomans upholstered in a rich fabric that complements the comforters. The bathroom is humongous, with a spa tub, a separate shower, double sinks with gold fixtures, and every amenity one could ever imagine. The word "wow" comes out of our mouths at the same time.

The staff member sees our reaction and says in English, "I hope these accommodations meet with your approval."

I attempt to show some restraint and respond, "Thank you, we'll be just fine here." As she closes the door, Hillary and I hug each other and giggle like two giddy teenagers, and Hillary exclaims, "This suite makes two of my apartments. Is this awesome or what?"

I chime in with, "Look at this bathroom! My God, this place gives a whole new meaning to the word 'extravagance.' I'm so glad we didn't go to the local hotel. I checked out photos online, and it can't hold a candle to this opulence."

It's now 9:30 p.m., and we're both weary from a long day of travel. We collapse on our beds, but when sleep begins beckoning us, I jump up and say to Hillary, "No, girlfriend, we can't rest now. We have to enjoy the feast."

Hillary looks at me and says, "I know, but I'm

dead tired and it's late. Can you let me have just ten minutes of sleep?"

In response, I grab her ankles and pull her out of the bed. She's laughing the entire time and catches herself before she tumbles to the floor. After freshening up, we join the rest of the party.

Pablo calls everyone together and serves each of us a glass of wine in a lovely, heavy, cut-crystal goblet. He makes a toast to our team, calling out each of our names, and joyfully announces how pleased he is to have us as his guests. When he finishes the toast, we all say in unison, "*¡Salud!*" We then enjoy the most luscious Mexican meal I've ever tasted, complete with homemade flour tortillas; delicious chicken, pork, and beef for tacos and fajitas; fresh salmon; and vegan selections. I must save room for dessert, which is an assortment of flan, churros, and fruit-filled empanadas. Pablo has outdone himself with attention to every detail.

After the meal, he sees we're all quite tired and directs the staff to show us back to our rooms. Before I leave, he addresses me: "Lucia, we look forward to chatting more in the morning and sharing the plans we have for your visit. For now, you all need to rest. Good night, and since tomorrow is Sunday, please sleep as late as you like."

I thank Pablo, and Hillary and I return to our suite. Once we're back there, I can tell Hillary is nervous about her problem, so I try to reassure her:

"Hey, my sister, sleep well, and remember, you have control over your problem."

Hillary nods but adds, "I agree, but I'll take the necessary precaution with my Depends, just in case." We prepare for bed and are both sound asleep as soon as our heads hit the pillows.

We awaken about three o'clock in the morning to what sounds like gunfire and loud yelling. Hillary and I both jump up, but we're not sure whether to try and peek out the windows or lock ourselves in the bathroom. We wisely opt for the bathroom. The gunfire continues for what seems like hours but in reality is only a few minutes. We hear screaming and shouting to stay in our rooms. I'm not sure if any member of our team is insane enough to go outside. We are in a state of total panic and just hold on to each other as Hillary begins to pray: "Lord, you said you would never leave us or forsake us. I take you at your word. Please keep all of us safe and free from harm and danger. Bless those who are protecting us from the evil ones. Thank you for your grace and mercy. Amen!"

The girl's prayers are powerful, because the gunfire and shouting immediately stop. There is an eerie silence, and then we can hear talking and people running around the grounds. We remain frozen in place in the bathroom. Suddenly, we hear loud knocking at our door, and a male voice that sounds like Pablo Castillo's starts shouting. "Lucia and Hillary, it's Pablo Castillo. Are you all right? Everything is under control, and it's safe for you to come out. Please open the door."

We look at each other, and I whisper to Hillary, "How do we know he's Pablo? Suppose he's one of the bad guys?"

The knocking continues and grows louder. Finally, we hear a key turn, and the door opens and I say aloud what was going through my head. "Oh my God, we should have listened to Mother Montgomery. I will never doubt or question her thoughts in the future." By this time, the footsteps are right outside the bathroom door and the Pablo sound-alike speaks again. "Lucia, you and Hillary are safe. Please open the door."

I yell out, "How do we know you're really Pablo?"

The man responds, "I assure you I'm Pablo. You should know my voice by now."

We're still not taking any chances, so I yell again, "Tell us something that happened when you last visited Sanger."

We hear him laugh. "Well, one member of my team who shall remain nameless made a comment in Spanish about liking beautiful Black sisters, and dear Hillary accepted the compliment in excellent Spanish."

We breathe a sigh of relief and then open the door. Thank God it really is Pablo. He gives us each a hug and explains what was behind the attack. "I recently dismissed several of my hired hands for stealing. They decided to seek revenge and, knowing my Sanger guests were coming, chose this time to launch an attack. I assure you that nothing like this has ever happened on my property, and it won't happen again. I got a heads-up call from one of the men seeking to reclaim his job about a possible attack but never thought it would actually happen. Nonetheless, my security team, one of the best worldwide, is always prepared for the unexpected, and anyone would have to be insane to launch an attack on my property. My men made sure that those guys never have the opportunity to attack my ranch, or any other ranch, for that matter."

We're still trembling, so Pablo continues to talk to us. "I'm so sorry you had this horrible experience. Words can't describe my embarrassment. I know you hear all of these bad things about Mexico in the States, but trust me, you're safer here than you are in most of the cities in the States. The rest of your team is safe and just as shaken as the two of you. I'm happy to move you to the hotel in town if you're no longer comfortable staying out here."

We look at each other, and I say to Hillary, "Who will protect us if we move from the ranch?" I'm also thinking, *Where will we find such luxury in town?* I make an executive decision. "I think we should stay here, but the rest of the team should weigh in on this decision." Hillary nods in agreement.

I tell Pablo, "We need to get with our team, first of all, to make sure they're okay. We will then make a collective decision as to whether we stay at the ranch or move into town." I suddenly realize we're in our pajamas and ask Pablo to excuse us while we change clothes.

The staff lead Hillary and me into a magnificent dining room, which seals the deal for me: we are staying at the ranch. The rest of the team is already there, and they look as if they've seen a million ghosts. It's very disturbing to see the fear on their faces. I think we all grasp the realization we're in a foreign country, far from the comforts and security of home. I can see they're all looking to me for reassurance and direction. I've got to step up right now and be the leader this team desperately needs.

"Listen, guys, this morning I was just as scared as each of you during the commotion. I'm now totally confident we're safe and won't let the actions of some disgruntled former employees destroy the work we've come here to achieve. However, if you're no longer comfortable here, we can move to a hotel in the city. We should be fine, but we won't have the Castillo security team with us. You need to know Pablo Castillo has assured me of our safety for the duration, and I believe him. Now, what are your thoughts?"

Jung speaks first: "Lucia, I'm the first to admit I have never been so scared in my entire life, but nothing is going to stop me from getting the work done on this project."

Lillian is next: "I agree with Jung. I actually peed in my pants last night, but I'm still in."

Hillary and I exchange secret glances. Then Ernie jumps in: "You can count on me, Lucia. I'm for staying at the ranch. I don't think we're safer at a hotel in the city. This may sound odd, but my room is off the hook and I think I want to enjoy this luxury for a while." We all laugh.

Everyone looks at Hillary then. She speaks as only Hillary can. "You know, I was scared beyond words and huddled with Lucia in a locked bathroom while all of the drama was going on outside. My mother has a host of people praying for us around the clock. The good thing is, the prayers of those righteous saints saw us through, and they're still praying for us. So I'm here for the long haul. Lucia selected each of us over other, equally competent staff, and we're going to make her and Sanger proud. I am so in, and after what we've experienced, nothing is going to stop us."

That's my girl! Love me some Hillary. I say, "Okay, it looks as if we're still on task. Fear is not an option for this team. Castillo Information Systems, the Sanger 'Fearless' Team is here to do business!"

Jung says, "I think the Sanger Fearless Team should become our secret name."

We laugh in agreement, then put our hands together like athletes do when their team is on a roll and shout, "To the Sanger Fearless Team!"

I add, "We're ready to finish this project with flying colors. Go, team!"

31 DARRYL

It Is Possible to Change

Today I completed my fifth session with Dr. Ike Thompson. Michael was right about Dr. Thompson. He has a way of reaching into the depths of an inner self I never knew existed. I feel totally comfortable opening up to him, and there's no doubt these sessions have probably been lifesaving. I didn't realize how deeply my high school years had scarred my heart with so much hate. The hardest part for me was coming to grips with having allowed my classmates to make me ashamed of the father I loved so much.

Charles was the primary target of my bitterness because he cleverly made up all the cruel jokes and rhymes about my father and caused me so much pain. I had a hard time facing up to both my hatred and my shame, but now I know I spent too much wasted energy waiting for the opportunity to get even with Charles, only to learn he also loved my father. His jealousy of Daddy's love for me and my family drove him to acts of cruelty. It's amazing how forgiveness frees you.

Oh, how I wish my father were here so I could ask for his forgiveness. He never knew how ashamed I was of his work and our poverty, but now I would let him know how much I regret not having respected his hard, honest labor. I would tell him how proud I am to have a loving and honorable man as my father who cared so much for his family. Now I understand why he was so content in spite of having had little money. I now know how generously he gave to others in spite of his poverty. His big heart, so full of love for others, was the core of his contentment. I never thought I'd ever want to be like my father, but it turns out he was rich in more ways than I could ever comprehend or achieve with my executive compensation.

I've focused my adult life on acquiring things to impress others and to avenge past wrongs. Hatred drained all of the love out of my heart. I want to bring love back into my life. I'd like to experience the joy Charles talked about in his letter.

My thoughts then drift to Hillary. She must think I'm the worst jerk on this earth. It's ironic that I've taken on the characteristics I most hated in my classmates. I'm ashamed of the way I've bullied and tormented Hillary. I'm her Charles Watson. She reminded me of the women who caused pain in my childhood, especially my father's sister, Aunt Laura. Aunt Laura had everything going her way financially and looked down her nose at our family.

I despised her for doing well while we were suffering financially. She never once offered to help. She would belittle my father at family gatherings with her embarrassing questions about his work. I once hoped she would drown when one of our family events was at the lake. I heard she cried the loudest at my father's funeral. I'm sure it was because of the guilt she felt. She's old and fragile now, and I've never reached out to her and, frankly, never will. Maybe the therapy will change my mind, but I doubt it.

Dr. Thompson asked me how Hillary reminded me of my aunt. I thought about it and recall Aunt Laura's pretty cocoa complexion. She was a beautiful, brown-skinned woman, and very intelligent. I recognized Hillary's beauty and intelligence when I first interviewed her, but all I could see was Aunt Laura, waiting to cause me pain. I transferred to Hillary the hatred I felt toward my aunt and my female classmates, for reasons I've yet to understand. I was determined to make her pay for the pain they all caused me. I had become consumed with hatred for all Black women. It didn't make sense, since I adored my mother. The mind is truly a complex organism. Dr. Thompson finally helped me see Hillary as Hillary, and not as Aunt Laura. At some point, I have to apologize to Hillary. I won't blame her if she tells me to go straight to hell. Little does she know, I've already been to hell and back in my warped state of being.

Cathy asked to have a meeting with me this morning, and I'll be disappointed but not surprised if she says she's quitting. I really like Cathy as my assistant and as a kind and caring human being. She's not the best assistant from a skills perspective, but she tries hard to please me and her work ethic is over the top. I believe she's also very loyal.

I can tell she's a bit nervous this morning by the way she's avoided eye contact with me. I might as well call her in now and get this over with. I speak with her over the intercom: "Cathy, do you mind if we have our meeting now? I know it's about a half hour early, but I have a few things I need to take care of, and now is a good time."

Cathy's nervousness is very evident when she walks into my office. "Mr. Kelsey, I'm sorry to take time out of your busy schedule, but there's something I want to share with you that's really bugging me."

I'm nervous but encourage Cathy to speak freely. "Cathy, whatever it is, please just be open with me. I don't ever want you to feel you can't talk to me."

She nods anxiously and says, "Well, this is a bit difficult because it involves one of our senior leaders and a Human Resources manager." She takes a deep breath. "About a month ago, Jim Waters called me into his office while you were on travel and asked me how I like working for you. He wanted to know if there had ever been any instances of unacceptable behavior. I asked him what he meant by 'unacceptable behavior.' He said, 'You know, sexual harassment.' I was speechless and asked him why he would ask such a thing. He said it's because you were so intent on hiring a pretty assistant."

Why, the dirty rat! I can't believe my ears, but I don't let Cathy see my anger as she continues. "I told Jim you have always treated me with the utmost respect and that I was surprised he'd asked such a question. He then said John Griffin had asked him to meet with me and ask the questions because he was concerned about my welfare."

Now things are falling into place. "Hmm, is that right? This is very disturbing to me."

Cathy continues, "I felt uncomfortable with his line of questioning, and I told Hillary about it. I know you don't like her, but she is such a wonderful person."

I try to correct Cathy: "I never said I didn't like Hillary."

She makes direct eye contact with me and says, "Sir, you've never said you don't like Hillary, but your body language and the words you use about her give you away. You don't treat her with respect, and you don't even want her coming into this area. I felt terrible having to tell her she couldn't come up here anymore. No one else besides Hillary has ever been told to stay away from this area. I know it hurt her feelings, but, as always, she was very professional and gracious because she knew I was your messenger.

"As a matter of fact, Mr. Kelsey, everyone knows you don't like her. I hope my openness isn't getting me in trouble."

I guess Michael was right after all. I can only imagine the things my coworkers say about me. I tell Cathy, "No, not at all. I appreciate your honesty. Please, go on."

"Well, Hillary said she overheard John and Jim a while back planning how they were going to bring you down. She was very concerned about you and told Lucia what she had heard. The two of them were trying to keep an eye on John and Jim to find out what they were up to. Lately, the Castillo project has had Lucia and Hillary working around the clock, so they no longer have time to monitor those two characters."

Cathy shifts nervously in her chair. "I'm telling you this because you've been the best boss I've ever had. You're one of the first bosses I haven't had to continuously fight off sexual advances from. In all honesty, I was fired from my last job because I wouldn't accept my boss's advances. I apologize for lying to you that I was laid off. I really appreciate your patience with my slow learning curve as I try to brush up on my skills to do a much better job. You aren't aware of this, but Hillary has been helping me come up to speed. I can't thank her enough for her kindness. If you got to know her, you would see she's someone very special. Maybe it will happen one day, but I'm not here to talk about Hillary. I thought you needed to know those guys are steadily plotting against you."

I'm moved by Cathy's concern for my welfare and say, "Thank you, Cathy. I can't tell you how much I appreciate your sharing this information with me. I admit I thought you asked for this meeting to tell me you were leaving. I'm not happy about what you've told me, but I'm thrilled it was not your resignation. You are an awesome assistant, and I appreciate all the things you do. Please forgive me if I've ever given the impression I take you for granted."

Tears are welling up in Cathy's eyes and begin to overflow. "Thank you, Mr. Kelsey."

It's time for some big changes in my interactions with Cathy, and I'd like to start today. "By the way, Cathy, let's stop this Mr. Kelsey stuff. Please call me Darryl."

She has a pensive look on her face as she says quietly and timidly, "Okay, Darryl."

I stand up and walk around my desk to where she is sitting. She looks confused, until I open my arms. She stands up hesitantly, and I give her a gentle hug and thank her once again. As she turns to go back to her desk, I add, "Oh, and thanks for your straight talk about my behavior with Hillary. I can assure you that you're about to see a change—a positive change—in my interactions with her."

Cathy turns and surprises me as she returns my hug. "Thanks, Mr....I mean Darryl. I'm sorry, I'll need a little time to get used to calling you by your first name." She smiles and walks out my office.

The things Cathy disclosed about those two slimeballs hit me right in the gut. I had a feeling I couldn't trust either of them, but I expected much more from Jim. They just can't leave well enough alone and seem to thrive on continuously stirring up trouble. I think I'll give them a taste of their own medicine. No, wait—I'd better talk to Michael about this. He's had to handle those two in the past when they tried to assassinate his character. They spread malicious rumors about his engaging in inappropriate conduct with young boys. Sanger should have gotten rid of them then, but good ol' Michael believed they could be rehabilitated and gave them another chance. He must know by now that rehabilitation isn't possible with those two.

I'll give Michael a call later today to see what we can do to address the two evil ones lurking among us, but before I do anything else, I've got to speak with Hillary. I buzz Cathy on the intercom to schedule a meeting with Hillary. Cathy pokes her head in my door and says, "Darryl, Hillary is at her desk. Shall I ask her to come up now?"

I hesitate for a moment. Whew, I've got to get

myself together for this conversation. What do you say to someone you've treated like dirt? Will she even listen to what I have to say? I guess I'll soon find out. "Yes," I answer, "please have her come on up."

Cathy buzzes me on the intercom to let me know Hillary has arrived. "Are you ready to see her?"

"Yes, please bring her in."

Hillary enters my office hesitantly; her apprehension about meeting with me is palpable. I reach out to shake her hand and ask her to take a seat at my round table. I pull out a chair next to hers. I don't want a desk to separate us during this conversation. I see the surprised look on Hillary's face, and I'm sure she's thinking about what transpired during her initial interview with me.

"Hillary, thank you for meeting with me on such short notice," I say. "I'm not sure how to start this conversation, but I want you to know how sorry I am for the way I've treated you since you arrived at Sanger. I was totally out of line during your interview with me. You more than met the qualifications for the position, but I treated you as if you had some contagious disease. I could give you an excuse for my behavior, but no, there is no acceptable excuse. I've acted like a complete jerk, and I hope you accept my apology."

Hillary pauses thoughtfully before responding, "Mr. Kelsey, I accept your apology. I was very curious about what this meeting was about, and, to be honest, I was expecting the worst. Thank you for offering an apology." She looks down at her hands and then back up at me. "If you don't mind, can you please share what it is about me that turned you off so quickly when we first met? It was as if you disliked me the minute I walked into your office. If I came across the wrong way or did something unknowingly, please tell me so I'm better aware of my behavior."

I take a deep breath to collect my thoughts. "Hillary, it was absolutely nothing you did wrong. The problem was totally with me. It's hard to explain, but I'll give you the short version for now. I had a rough childhood growing up in a poor but loving family. I wasn't the Darryl Kelsey you see today. I was the overweight, dark-skinned, dorky kid everyone picked on. One guy in particular and all of the Black girls gave me a hard time. At least to me it seemed like all of them. I also had an aunt whom I loathed because she wasn't very kind to my family. There's no valid excuse to explain my behavior, but for some reason I immediately transferred a lot of the pent-up anger to you that I harbored against those Black women.

"You were here and an easy target for the poisons I've carried for so many years. Maybe one day I can share more with you. I hope this explanation—though I don't offer it as an excuse—is acceptable for now."

Hillary is looking at me, but I can tell her mind is in another, distant place. "Thanks, Mr. Kelsey. I appreciate your sharing something so personal with me. It will stay right here in this room."

I look into Hillary's eyes and get a glimpse of the inner beauty others see. This is the Hillary I've heard so much about, and she really is special. "Hillary, you have modeled the utmost professionalism even when I've been disrespectful to you. I know I don't deserve it, but thank you for your heart of forgiveness. Before you leave, I'd like to ask one more favor." She gives me a quizzical look. "If you don't mind, I'd like for us to make a fresh start. We can begin with you calling me Darryl, instead of Mr. Kelsey."

Hillary looks at me with amazement. "Darryl, you don't have to apologize any further. We all make mistakes at one time or another. It's just part of life. I'm happy with the fresh start, and we'll let the past stay in the past."

"Thank you, Hillary," I say. "That means a lot to me. By the way, I heard your project team had a very interesting time in Mexico."

She laughs and says, "Yes, interesting it was. In spite of one small incident, it was the right thing for us to go there and get a firsthand look at the Castillo operation. They're a class act, and Mr. Castillo was the perfect host."

"That's good to hear. As a leadership team, we

have to apologize to the team for not doing our due diligence in checking out the accommodations more thoroughly before sending you into a potentially hostile environment. I'm thankful none of you was injured and all of you returned safely."

Hillary says reassuringly, "There's no way anyone from Sanger could have known about the situation, and Mr. Castillo's team handled everything very quickly. I have to admit we were scared to death when our little incident happened, but with Lucia's leadership, everything stayed on track. Our team was determined to fulfill our mission during our visit to the Castillo facility. Lucia feels we have a much better grasp of their expectations now. We've also built a solid bond with the Castillo team."

I nod as Hillary gets up to leave and then turns back to say something else. "Darryl, I want to thank you for allowing me to participate on the team."

I appreciate her show of appreciation, but I also want to be truthful and not take undeserved credit. "Hillary, you may already know this, but I didn't want you on the team. It was Michael who advocated so strongly for you, and only then did I relent. He deserves all the credit, not me."

Hillary nods. "I appreciate Michael's advocacy, but I also know if you hadn't relented, I wouldn't have been able to participate, so my thanks stand."

We both smile, and I again express my appreciation to Hillary. "I can't thank you enough for your graciousness. I'm already enjoying our new start. By the way, Cathy thinks the world of you, and I've discovered she's an excellent judge of character." I stand to shake Hillary's hand and walk with her to the door.

"Darryl, isn't there something else you want to ask me?"

I'm puzzled by the question. "No, we've covered what I wanted to discuss."

"Oh, Cathy told me she shared with you about John and Jim. I thought you might want to know about the conversation I overheard."

I should probably back away from that topic. "I wasn't going to bring it up, because it's not why I wanted to meet with you. Raising the incident would also make my outreach seem a bit self-serving and disingenuous."

Hillary hesitates for a moment and says, "Thank you for that; it means a lot. You should know those two are really after you, so I suggest you watch your back. You probably aren't aware, but Jim has been recording your conversations with him, especially about the type of person you wanted to hire for your executive assistant. I don't believe in spreading gossip, but some things are wrong and need to be brought to light."

"Thanks, Hillary. I appreciate this feedback, and I will watch my back."

She looks at me with a twinkle in her eyes and

says, "You should know there are others who are watching with you."

I give her a quick hug, which takes her by complete surprise, and she leaves my office. She can rest assured those two snakes will have a date with destiny real soon. I can see Hillary giving Cathy a thumbs-up when she passes her desk.

32 HILLARY

God Never Fails!

I'm sitting here waiting for Lucia to join me for lunch, and I can't wait to tell her about my meeting with Darryl this morning. I've already ordered for her, because she's ordered the same item on the menu each of the zillion times we've come here. Can you believe it? Mr. Darryl Kelsey invited me to a meeting and apologized for his behavior toward me. God, you are something else. This was a miracle if I've ever seen one. I'm happy to have a fresh start with Darryl, and I hope we might even become friends. Something led to this change, and I know it's answered prayer. Today I saw the man I hoped to see when I first went through the interview process. I have to thank Cathy for her kind words about me. We've become friends, and I'm glad I reached out to her, even if at first it was to see if the two snakes were using her to get to Darryl. Wow, I'm calling him Darryl with no reservations—never thought that would happen in a million years.

Lucia flashes her pearly-white smile as she joins

me, and we give each other a hug. Our food orders arrive just as she sits down.

"Girl, you won't believe what happened to me this morning," I say.

Lucia laughs. "You mean your meeting with Darryl?"

"How did you find out?"

"News travels faster than lightning around that place."

"I'm sorry, my sister—I should have let you tell me. Anyway, Darryl mentioned it to Michael, and Michael told me about it. Darryl has also scheduled a meeting with me to get an update on the Castillo project and to learn more about our little fiasco at the Castillo ranch. I like the new Darryl."

I probably say too quickly, "I do, too. He asked me to call him Darryl, instead of Mr. Kelsey." For some reason, I realize I'm smiling when I mention Darryl's name.

Lucia gives me one of those *I know what you're thinking* looks, then suddenly grimaces as she changes the conversation to the evil twosome. "I understand Darryl is aware of the schemes of Satan's two brothers. I hope they finally get what's coming to them. Those two put a capital 'E' in 'evil.'"

I shake my head. "They'll come up with some lame excuse for why they were targeting Darryl, and nothing will happen to them. After all, they're two white males and their sins are forgiven repeatedly.

Now, if they were two Hispanic or Black brothers, they would have been out of Sanger in a hot minute. Don't forget, their target is also Black, so what's the big deal with bringing down one more Black man?"

Lucia looks at me as if she can't believe her ears. "My sister, I haven't heard you talk like this before. I didn't know you had a cynical bone in your body. Something's struck a nerve with you."

I'm surprised at how quickly my mood changed from elation to indignation when Lucia brought up the fate of the evil twins, but I admit, "Maybe so. I see too many minority and women leaders removed from their positions at the drop of a hat, and yet white male leaders get second and third chances before any action is taken against them. I know there are exceptions, but very few."

Lucia frowns and says, "I strongly believe those two are on a short rope, but we'll see. Anyway, all of this talk about the two evil ones is ruining my appetite, so let's change the subject."

I nod in agreement and say, "Lucia, I want to thank you again for adding me to the team."

She waves her hand. "You've thanked me enough, so stop it. You deserved to be on the team, and you're doing an amazing job. I want you to start acting like you are worthy of the opportunities coming your way and not behave as if someone's doing you a special favor. You are a smart and very talented professional, so quit being so subservient and show the confidence I know you have."

Lucia's right, and I tell her so. "I do feel I'm doing a great job on the team and adding value to this project. You're really fortunate to have me as a team member."

Lucia laughs. "Okay, Ms. Wonderful, don't carry the confidence thing *too* far. I hope I'm not creating a monster."

Suddenly, someone walks over to our table and greets us warmly but hesitantly. "Hi, Lucia and Hillary. Don't you just love this place? It's one of my favorite restaurants."

We sneak a quick glance at each other, and Lucia says, "Hi, Sheryl. Funny meeting you here." I'm sure Sheryl can feel the arctic air surrounding Lucia's greeting.

Sheryl responds, "I love coming here because the lively atmosphere always gives me a lift. Do you mind if I join you?"

Lucia and I are both surprised by this request, but I say, "Oh, please, join us." Lucia cuts her eyes at me, clearly communicating, *Are you out of your ever-loving mind?* I ignore her dagger look and begin talking to Sheryl. "How are things with you?"

I can see tears beginning to form as Sheryl responds. "I know I'm intruding but just felt the need to talk to somebody and saw the two of you.

If my presence is making you uncomfortable, especially you, Lucia, then I can leave."

Lucia's heart is a lot bigger than any animosity she has toward Sheryl, and her next remark reflects that: "No, Sheryl, please don't leave. You're right about my discomfort and surprise when you asked to join us. You've not had much to say to me for some time, but let's put that aside. I want you to stay."

Sheryl struggles for a response and thanks Lucia. She then takes a deep breath as the waiter hands her a menu, and says, "I know there are rumors around the office about an affair between John and me. I take full responsibility for making some bad decisions in my relationship with John, but, to set the record straight, I haven't had sex with him. We've done some heavy petting, but that's it. Even though I haven't let him go any further, I'm so ashamed of my behavior in this situation. You have to understand that my husband's employment is unstable, and with two children, I desperately need to work. I'm fortunate to have a great job with Sanger, and I don't want to lose it. To be honest with you, I despise John with a passion, but I'm totally defenseless against his advances. I've threatened to report him to Human Resources, but he laughs because he knows Jim Waters is one of his best buddies."

Lucia doesn't buy Sheryl's pity party. "Sheryl, I can't imagine being intimate with the likes of John

Griffin. He was overheard referring to you as a sex slave. If you can't go to that slimeball Jim, then go to Glenn Hendricks. There are laws against sexual harassment, and Glenn will go to bat for you."

Sheryl looks at Lucia with both surprise and maybe a tinge of anger. "I'm surprised you're suggesting I go to Human Resources. You complained about discrimination in your promotion, and what did it get you? Nothing! I know you think I didn't support you, but you're wrong—I tried my best. John told me if I persisted about your promotion, he would have me fired. You know, I was reprimanded because of the promise I made to you. I had every intention of keeping that promise. The good old boys run the show here, and I've faced up to the fact that as a woman at Sanger, I have no power."

I'm cringing at the thought of any intimate contact with that old buzzard, and I suddenly feel sorry for Sheryl. However, it's time for her to step up and get this five-hundred-pound gorilla off her back, so I offer a suggestion. "Sheryl, I think you will see some major changes in Sanger's leadership attitudes toward your situation. You can't let this kind of harassment continue, and Lucia and I will support you in standing up to John."

If looks could kill, Lucia gives me one that means instant death. She opens her mouth to speak, but I don't give her a chance. "I think you should go directly to Michael Dunlap. He's straight up, and he won't tolerate this or any other form of harassment. I trust him to do what's right by you. You deserve better, and you have to stand up to John."

Sheryl looks at me, but her thoughts seem to be taking her to another place in the crevices of her mind. I'm sure she's having an internal conversation as she processes my suggestion. When she speaks, her voice is barely above a whisper. "Hillary, you're willing to go with me? I thank you for that. I'm scared the whole thing will backfire on me, and I can't afford to lose my job."

I want to reassure her, but Lucia begins to speak. "Sheryl, one of my favorite quotes from Dr. Martin Luther King is 'A man can't ride your back unless you bend over.' It's time for you to stop bending over and stand tall. First of all, sexual harassment is illegal, and so is any form of retaliation. We'll both go with you to file your complaint, as I believe it will help to have two other women with you. It's time for John to get what he's deserved for some time, and that's a pink slip."

Sheryl perks up and says, "Okay, I will do it if you both are with me."

I respond, "We're with you all the way, and I know other women will also support you." I put my hand out, as the Sanger Fearless Team did when we agreed to stay at Pablo's ranch in Mexico. Sheryl places her hand on top of mine, and Lucia places her hand on top of Sheryl's. I proclaim, "We will slay this dragon!"

Sheryl and Lucia repeat my words: "We will slay this dragon!" Lucia and I stand up and have a group hug with Sheryl. When we sit back down, Sheryl looks at the menu and makes a selection. As the three of us enjoy a delicious meal together, I'm glad to see her looking much more relaxed.

33 DARRYL

The Big Showdown

ichael and I have scheduled meetings with John and Jim separately to see what we can find out about their latest antics. John wanted to know what the meeting was about. I had Cathy tell him it's a personnel matter we need his assistance to resolve.

As we're waiting for John, Michael shakes his head and says, "I can't believe those two characters are at it again. They just don't get it."

I nod my head in agreement. "Well, it'll be interesting to see if they'll say the same things separately as when they're together."

Cathy pops her head in and says John is on his way. I ask her to show him in when he gets here. When he walks in with his usual jovial but pretentious manner, he says, "Hey, Boss; hi, Michael. What's up?"

Michael nods for me to do the talking. "John, please have a seat. We have a few questions to ask you about a personnel matter you may have some background on. I understand Jim had a meeting with my assistant at your request. One of the questions Jim asked Cathy is whether I have ever sexually harassed her."

John turns red and says, "Jim asked her *what?* I have no idea what led him to suggest such a thing."

"We're not sure, which is why we're asking you. Jim told Cathy you were concerned for her welfare, since I wanted a pretty woman for my assistant."

John stands up and says, "Look, I didn't ask Jim to imply you were harassing Cathy. He overstepped his bounds and was way out of line. I'll have a talk with Jim and set him straight."

I motion for John to sit back down. "No, John, *I'll* talk with Jim. Let's set the record straight: I have spoken with Jim about what I'd like to see in my assistant. Mind you, it's no different than what you and others request when you're hiring staff."

As John shifts in his chair, I say, "By the way, I understand the two of you have been engaged in some serious planning to orchestrate my demise."

John really looks nervous now. "What planning? Someone is feeding you a bunch of baloney. You're my boss—why would I want to take you down?"

"Good question, John, and it's exactly the question I have. You and Jim were overheard sharing your plans to take me down. I'm not sure what actions the two of you have in mind, so perhaps you can explain it to me. The two of you have spent a lot of company time over the years trying to sabotage people here."

Michael speaks now: "Yes, and I can say from firsthand experience how treacherous your actions can be."

I'm enjoying seeing John sweat, as he says, "Look, Boss, I don't know what plans you're talking about. I've always been a loyal employee and have the utmost respect for you. And, Michael, the incident with you was a little misunderstanding. I'm surprised you're bringing it up now, since it happened almost two years ago."

I can't help but smile. "Okay, John, I think we're finished here for the time being. I'll get back with you shortly."

As John stands to leave, he says, "Believe me, Boss, this whole thing is a big misunderstanding." At this point, it's comical watching John's ingratiating behavior. I think he realizes that I'm no fool and definitely onto his antics.

"You're right, John, a very big misunderstanding, and don't worry—we'll get to the bottom of this and clear it up once and for all." I get up to show John out of the office and then hesitate. "One more thing before you leave: I hear there's also an issue with one of our female leaders being referred to as a 'sex slave.' I understand it involves you and Sheryl."

John's eyes look as if they're going to pop out of his head. "This has gone too far. Sheryl is on my staff, and our relationship is a working one only. Nothing more. Anyone who implies differently is a bold-faced liar. You hear me? A liar! I'd like to know who's spreading these false rumors."

"Okay, John, I'm sure we'll get to the bottom of all these issues. Thanks for coming up, and I'll be in touch with you."

After John walks out of my office, Michael shakes his head and says, "John is a piece of work. He's behind this mess, and he knows it. Now he wants to throw Jim under the bus, which is where they both belong."

I nod in agreement. "It's time to deal with these two, but first let's see what the other evil twin has to say." As if on cue, Cathy's on the intercom, saying Jim has arrived. I tell her to send him in.

Jim looks nervous when he enters the office and takes a seat. "Hi, Mr. Kelsey. Hi, Michael. What's going on?"

"Jim, there is a matter I'd like to discuss with you. I understand you had a meeting with my assistant and were concerned about whether I had sexually harassed her. What happened to make you think I would sexually harass my assistant?"

Jim shifts in his seat. "I didn't think you had harassed her. John wanted to be sure Cathy was doing okay. You know how you like attractive white women to apply for your executive assistant position."

Jim gives me a look that says, *If I'm going down, so are you.* "You're right in one respect, Jim: I have favored attractive assistants, but I never said she had to be white. In fact, you surmised I wanted an attractive assistant and are just as complicit, since you referred only attractive white females for my position." There's no way I'm giving John or anyone else the satisfaction of admitting that I wanted to hire only a white assistant. I didn't actually say it, even if I thought it. There's a big difference between the two.

"By the way, Jim," I continue, "are you recording this conversation?"

Jim looks like a kid with his hand caught in the cookie jar. "I would never record a conversation. What makes you think I would do such a thing?" His eyes begin to twitch as the lies come pouring out of his mouth.

"You were overheard telling John about having recorded our conversations. I don't understand why you of all people, as an HR leader, would do such a thing. I distinctly recall a section in the employee handbook that clearly states the recording of a conversation without the other party's knowledge is against company policy. Such an infraction is also subject to disciplinary action, up to and including termination. Were you planning to use the recordings as one of the ways you and John would take me down?"

Jim almost squeals his protest. "'Take you down'? What are you talking about?"

"Don't look so surprised, Jim. You and John were overheard planning my demise."

He's really squirming now. "Your *demise*? You've got to be kidding."

Michael can no longer hold his tongue. "Jim, you and John have been two of the most vile snakes at Sanger, and you've been here far too long, causing misery for a lot of people. It's time for you both to go."

Jim laughs. "Go? Are you kidding me? You can't get rid of me—I'm Human Resources! I know you have no legitimate cause for my termination. Anyway, if I go, then Mr. Darryl Kelsey also goes. I have the phone recordings to show he's engaged in discriminatory and sexist hiring practices."

Michael laughs. "Joke's on you, Mr. Human Resources—what phone recordings? The IT team just did a major purge of the phone system because of system overload, so anything you recorded has been erased. You have nothing!"

Jim's eyes turn a fiery red as he yells, "I'll sue you guys. John will join me, because he can't stand either of you." Perfect timing again: John walks back into the room, and I ask him to take a seat.

"John, Jim was just saying he's going to sue us and you will join him."

John looks at Jim with disbelief. "What the hell are you talking about? I have no intention of suing anyone. Are you nuts? Darryl is my boss, and you're talking crazy."

Jim is furious. "Oh, so *now* you're acting as if you're loyal to Darryl as your boss. You hate his guts, and you were the one who told me to question Cathy. Don't you dare try to come across as Mr. Innocent."

Michael and I are enjoying the exchange between the evil twins, but I've had enough of these two. "Listen, guys, I think it's best both of you get the hell out of my office. We'll decide how to address this situation through the leadership council. And Jim, I think you're aware of at-will employment. Just remember that when you cite all of your HR knowledge. In fact, you both are on paid administrative leave until we make a decision about your employment."

Michael suggests I call Glenn Hendricks in HR to handle this matter. I agree, knowing Glenn took a stand for Hillary and is known for his balanced advocacy for both employees and the company. Cathy gets Glenn on the phone, and I explain the situation to him. He seems to be quite happy to take on this matter. I'm sure he knows better than most the shenanigans of the evil twins. We'll figure out a way to get rid of them, even if we have to give them a few months of severance pay, which happens a lot in the corporate world. Corporate leaders who have acted inappropriately or exercised poor judgment waive their rights to sue and go away quietly with fat wallets. It will be worth every penny to get these two fools out of Sanger.

Michael suggests we call in Sheryl to further discuss the sexual harassment matter. I initially agree but then decide Glenn or someone else in Human Resources should speak with her. We want to make sure she feels comfortable and protected in telling her story, and that won't happen if Michael and I talk to her. She may be key in John and Jim's termination, without severance pay, if she confirms incidents of sexual harassment. Jim would be equally complicit if sexual harassment were substantiated and he knew about it and took no action against it. Michael agrees this is the right direction to take.

We both feel confident and take much pleasure in the fact that, regardless of the result of the sexual harassment investigation, John and Jim will never return to Sanger.

34 HILLARY

All's Well That Ends Well

What a beautiful rainy day in paradise. I love to hear the melodic sound of raindrops dancing against my windows. My eyelids are heavy and fighting to avoid opening this morning. The drizzle makes me want to stay in bed, but not today.

I feel around my bed and, instead of dampness, find only dryness to greet me on this special morning. Hallelujah! Dr. Bellamy has been amazing with my treatment. I've learned to manage my stress in a way that makes my bladder happy. I've prayed for this day for so many years. It's especially awesome since today is the big day when the Castillo team will return and hopefully award a major contract to Sanger.

I went through Dr. Bellamy's stress-management routine before bed, closing my eyes and imagining I was on a beach at a luxurious and tranquil resort. I could hear the waves and feel the warmth of the sun. I cleared my mind of everything that causes stress and anxiety. In spite of that mental respite and my efforts to remain optimistic, I had this irksome feeling I'd wake up to my usual wet sheets. But not today!

Today is a great day, and, Lord, I thank you for bringing me this far. I think I'll wear my new form-fitting slacks and matching short jacket. I don't mind showing off my new figure; I've lost twenty-five pounds since I joined Sanger and started a new workout routine. When Darryl complimented me yesterday morning, I felt an unexpected rush of warmth flowing throughout my body. His encouraging words had me smiling inside and out. His exact words were, "Hillary, you've got it going on, girl. Love your new look."

I thanked him and flashed my *I know it* smile. It's good to see Darryl actually happy and engaging in conversation with Sanger employees whom he never would have talked to in the past. Everyone's talking about his positive change. He's gone from a minus-ten to a plus-ten on the likability scale.

Okay, enough daydreaming. I need to get my butt out of bed and ready for work. Lucia has scheduled an eight fifteen internal meeting prior to the Castillo team meeting.

We're all on pins and needles as we prepare and await Castillo's final decision. We've worked hard, and Lucia has shown she's an outstanding leader. There's been strong mutual support, not the cut-throat antics of some of the dysfunctional teams I've encountered at other companies.

I called my mother on the way to work, and her words of encouragement infused me with positive energy. She spent most of the time telling me how proud she is of the work I'm doing. She was especially pleased when I told her about the new Darryl. She was silent for a moment, and I know what was going through my mother's head. Before she could speak, I said, "No, mom, I'm not interested in dating Darryl, so don't even go there."

I could feel the wheels turning in her heard as she said, "Oh, sweetheart, I wasn't thinking such a thing. You know I prayed with my prayer partners for him to change, and maybe now we can move to the next level in our praying for Darryl."

"Mom, I love you, but don't you dare do what I think you're about to do. I'll talk to you later." I had to laugh because I knew she would start calling her prayer group as soon as she hung up the phone.

By eight fifteen, Lucia and the rest of our team have all gathered to go over our presentation assignments and answer any last-minute questions. I'm so proud of my girl. She has proven if you give an assignment to a talented person, along with the authority to act, it's amazing what she can accomplish. Just think, all this time, Sanger has missed out on the contributions of an outstanding leader because of her accent. I wish there were more leaders like Michael Dunlap, who makes assignments based on his staff's demonstrated abilities and their potential, bolstered by his high expectations. He creates an environment for his staff to stretch and grow in. He doesn't care about a person's race, gender, accent, or sexual orientation. It's a blessing to work for and with him.

Lucia starts the meeting by thanking the team. "My wonderful teammates, words can't express how special you are and how much you mean to me and to Sanger. You have gone above and beyond the call of duty, even in the midst of real danger, to get this job done. I am so proud of each of you. Okay, I've got to take a deep breath because my tear ducts are beginning to act up. I just can't thank you enough for your commitment, your integrity, your loyalty, and your many talents."

Jung speaks up: "Lucia, I think I speak on behalf of the team, the Sanger Fearless Team, in saying you are an awesome leader. I believe we'd follow you to hell. Hey, wait—we almost went there during our trip to Mexico. All jokes aside, we appreciate the opportunity you've given us to showcase our talents individually and collectively."

The rest of us nod in agreement. Lucia wipes away a tear. "Thanks, guys. Now, do we have everything in place for our presentations? Are they all loaded and ready to go? Did we do a final computer check?"

We give affirmative nods to all of Lucia's questions, before she continues, "Jung, you'll follow my introductory remarks; Ernie, you're next; then Lillian; and Hillary brings up the rear. Are we ready for showtime?"

We recite in unison, "We're ready!" and proceed to the conference room.

The number of Sanger leaders in the room, including the company CEO, is a complete surprise. The Castillo team is happy to see us, and we exchange hugs and pats on the back with them. We can see looks of approval from our leaders as well.

Darryl kicks off the meeting by thanking the Castillo team for their presence and thanking Lucia and our team for the quality and quantity of work we've put into this project. After he completes the Sanger leadership introductions, he asks Pablo Castillo to introduce his team, then turns the meeting over to Lucia.

Lucia really works the room. "This has been one of the most challenging and yet rewarding projects for the team and for me. We've learned so much, and I want to thank Darryl and Michael for giving us this opportunity. I also want to thank the Castillo team for inviting us to their facility in Cuernavaca, Mexico. We had a wonderful time and learned so much about the Castillo operations. As a result, we are confident the project recommendations are better aligned with Castillo Information Systems' needs and expectations.

"We will now hear from the team members

on their specific area of responsibility. First, allow me to introduce the team members in the order of their presentations: Jung Chin, Lillian Brown, Ernie Morales, and Hillary Montgomery. I will close with an overall project summary. At this time, I'd like for Jung to present the findings in regard to Castillo's system support needs." Lucia gets a nice round of applause; then Jung makes his presentation, followed by Lillian and Ernie.

When my turn comes, I ask the Sanger leaders if it's okay to make my presentation in Spanish because there are some terms the Castillo team is more familiar with in their native tongue. Lucia agrees to translate for the Sanger people. I provide copies of my presentation in English to the Sanger leaders and in Spanish to the Castillo team. I can see the CEO's look of surprise, since he wasn't in previous meetings where I demonstrated my fluency in Spanish. The other leaders look very confident that they'll see a repeat performance today of my earlier success.

When I finish my presentation, I see Lucia, Darryl, and Michael all beaming with pride. The Castillo team and Sanger leaders give our team rousing applause after Lucia provides the summary and answers final questions.

Pablo Castillo is up next, and he acknowledges our team in a most powerful way. "I want to thank Sanger for sending one of the best project teams

I've ever had the pleasure of working with to our facility. Lucia has exemplified exceptional leadership, and I've never seen a more committed group. What impressed me most was when the team had a pretty harrowing experience—and, I regret, were fearful for their lives at one point on my ranch—but when they could easily have returned home, they chose to stay and get the job done instead. They never complained or once brought up the incident during the rest of their stay. They worked tirelessly for long hours to learn our processes and procedures and ensure the contract reflected our needs and our demands. On behalf of the Castillo team, we are delighted to enter into a five-year contract with Sanger for the amount of one hundred fifty million dollars per year."

All the Sanger leaders cheer, and our team is ecstatic. Pablo continues, "There is one stipulation to finalizing the contract. We want to have—no, we *insist* on having—the same team manage the contract. Of course, Sanger leadership will have to add the appropriate support staff. I firmly believe the relationship we've developed with Lucia and her team will ensure a successful venture. If possible, we'd also like the team to make monthly visits to our facility, which we will cover separately from this contract. It's a pleasure to begin this new venture with Sanger."

Darryl gets up to speak. "Thank you, Pablo, and

we're excited about and appreciative of the opportunity to work with Castillo. Lucia and her team will continue working on this project. We will provide the appropriate supplemental staff to support this effort. I know you all have a plane to catch, so, on behalf of Sanger, we again thank you for this incredible opportunity."

Pablo and his team stand up and go around the room, shaking hands. When Pablo gets to me, he whispers, "My beautiful sister, I'd love for you to spend quality time at the ranch whenever your time permits. I will send my private jet to pick you up— just let me know. I think you are amazing."

I blush and say to Pablo, "Mr. Castillo, I'm very flattered by your invitation." He winks, and we say good-bye.

The Sanger leadership team stays in the room and asks Lucia and the rest of the team to remain as well. Darryl introduces Andrew Pastocco, the CEO of Sanger, who speaks to our team. "Lucia, Jung, Lillian, Ernie, and Hillary, you have done an incredible job, and the Castillo contract is a huge win for Sanger. I'm trying to find the right words to say to you, but they're hard to come by. First, I'd like to congratulate each of you on your new role: Lucia, as vice president of South American Ventures; Jung and Lillian, as directors of Castillo Contract Administration; Ernie, as director of Computer Systems, Castillo Ventures; and Hillary, as director of

Customer Relations for South American Ventures. You will all report to Lucia. I also have the pleasure of passing an envelope to each of you with Sanger's monetary recognition of your contributions. You have made us all proud, and we are grateful for your work and the fruits of your labor." Mr. Pastocco shakes hands and embraces each of us as he hands over envelopes imprinted with our names.

Wow, this was so unexpected, but I'm now soaring. Michael gives each of us a hug, and so does Darryl. I love the cologne Darryl is wearing, and his hug lingers a bit longer with me than it does with the others. Lucia notices, of course, and exchanges a quick wink with me when no one is looking. That girl—she's just like my mother.

What a day! I am absolutely exhausted when I get home. Amid all the things that went on for the remainder of my workday, I didn't get a chance to open my envelope. I tear it open now and almost faint. Inside is a check for $60,000. I just run around the room screaming, crying, and thanking God for this tremendous blessing.

My phone rings, and I see Lucia's name on the caller ID. Before I can say a word, she blurts out, "Girl, did you open your envelope? Is this crazy or what? First, I'm now a vice president, and second, I was given a one-hundred-thousand-dollar bonus! I am doing a happy dance right now. How about you?"

"Lucia, thank you, thank you, and don't tell me to stop. You give a whole new meaning to 'friend.' You put your neck on the line for me to be a part of the team. Girl, I'm doing a boogie-woogie dance because I was given a sixty-thousand-dollar bonus and my bed was dry when I awoke this morning. Heaven has truly opened up and smiled on me—on both of us. I have to call my mother and thank her for all those powerful prayers. I'm so happy right now. My heart is about to burst from so much joy."

Before we hang up, Lucia suggests we take a couple days off and spend a long weekend shopping in Chicago. Sounds great to me. I love Chicago, and for the first time, I can go and have real money to spend. As I remove my jacket, a funny thing happens: a whiff of Darryl's cologne caresses my face, and a warm feeling engulfs my body. I need to call my mother right away and tell her to stop those prayers for Darryl, because they're beginning to affect me as well. Hmm, maybe that's not such a bad thing after all.

Acknowledgments

After several years of creating this book in my head, I thank God for giving me the ability and confidence to put my thoughts on paper. God has blessed me in so many ways, and I give Him all the praise for his goodness and unconditional love. Without Him, this book would not have been possible.

It's truly been a blessing to spend quality, uninterrupted time—for the first time in thirty-five years—to pursue my passion for writing without having to compete with the demands of a full-time corporate leadership position. I'm thankful for the many years I spent in corporate America, because those opportunities and challenges helped shape some of the stories in this book. It's amazing how other stories evolved from life experiences of family, friends, and colleagues, as well as my vivid imagination.

I'm especially thankful for the tremendous support I've received from family and friends. I can't tell you how often I've heard, "Girl, where are you with the book? When is the book going to be finished? Did you write today? Hurry up, girl—I need my book!" Those continuous words of encouragement have kept me focused and on task. My wonderful husband, Fred C. Jenkins, Jr., has been my most ardent cheerleader for over forty-eight years. He is truly the love of my life. I thank my sons, Kevin and Fred Jenkins III, for also being their mother's cheerleaders, along with my daughter-in-law, Cristina Roman Jenkins, and my wonderful grandsons, Chawn Jenkins, Tyler Pierce, Cedric Shaneyfelt, Ché Jenkins, Kevin Jenkins, Jr., and Jadon Jenkins.

I have the most awesome family ever, and I can't thank them enough for their encouragement and support in whatever I seek to accomplish. Thanks to my sisters and brothers, who inspire me in so many ways: Laura Peppetta and her husband, Andrew; Frank Bell and his wife, Cynthia; Ike Bell, Edith Kelsey, and her husband, Lemont; Catherine Fisher and Lucy Bell. I must send special thanks to my nieces and nephews and their families for their strong words of encouragement, especially Tesha Bell, Hillary White-Nash, Pastor Glenn R. Shields, Yvette Shields, Tamara Kirk, Famous Kirk, Jr., and Linda White.

There's no way I could go on without mentioning my dear friends who have been over the top in supporting me through this journey. Thank you, Carmen Marriott, Doris Ford, Jimmy and Lillian Thompson, Vivian Montgomery, Gail Dunlap, James and Doris Lee, Sally Murray, Rosetta Bullock, Joe and Felicia Jackson, Challis Lowe, Ruth Brinkley, Doris Ford, Bob Perez, Nancy Ginger-Ivens, Collier and Wyllstyne Hill, Elise Collins Shields, Monica Casper, and too many others to name who supported me in some way. I can't forget my Sabino Canyon walking partners: Liz Whitaker, Suzanne Jacoby, Gail Paulin, Robyn Allsman, and Deb Turner. I love and appreciate you all.

What a blessing to have my dear friend Joe Jackson develop the design concept for the book cover. Joe is a talented photographer and generously shares his many gifts to enrich our community.

Special thanks to my publisher, Wheatmark, for their tremendous support in getting my book published.

Lastly, hugs, smiles, and many thanks to my wonderful editor, Annie Tucker. This would have been a very difficult journey without her. I also thank She Writes Press for their support and especially for introducing me to Annie.

About the Author

Daisy M. Jenkins, Esq., is president of Daisy Jenkins & Associates and a retired human resources executive with over thirty-three years of experience at Fortune 500 companies. She has written several articles published by *The Root*, Ebony.com, and the *Huffington Post*, including "Pro Athletes, Big Winners and Losers When the Career Clock Goes to Zero"; "The Roberts Court Gave Affirmative Action Its Last Rites, It's Up to Us to Revive It"; "Justice Department's Anti-Smoking Efforts Exclude Black Media"; and "Teaching Black Girls to Be Beautiful." She is an education advocate and mentors diverse professionals across the country. Jenkins and her adorable husband, Fred, have been married for forty-eight years and have two sons and six grandsons.

CPSIA information can be obtained at www.ICGtesting.com
Printed in the USA
BVOW04s0208120315

391223BV00002B/41/P

9 781627 872065